THE SEA CLOAK

The Sea Cloak

Nayrouz Qarmout

Translated by Perween Richards

Title story translated by Charis Olszok

First published in Great Britain by Comma Press, 2019.
www.commapress.co.uk

A CIP catalogue record of this book is available from the British Library.

ISBN-10 1905583788
ISBN-13 978-1-90558-378-2

This book has been selected to receive financial assistance from
English PEN's 'PEN Translates' programme.

The publisher gratefully acknowledges the support of Arts Council England.

Printed and bound in England by Clays Ltd, Elcograf S.p.A

Contents

The Sea Cloak

ONCE AGAIN, SHE RETREATED into the past, to a sprawling camp buzzing with children playing marbles and forming teams for a game of 'Jews and Arabs'. She saw herself aged ten, wearing a short dress and skipping with a group of girls in a sandy alleyway shadowed by sheets of corrugated iron. She dropped the rope abruptly as a little boy snatched a butterfly clip from her hair and ran off with it. She raced after him. Her shoes flew from her small feet but she kept running, oblivious to everything except the sand on the ground that soon carried her to a pathway littered with stones. She tripped and fell. Her dress was stained with dirt but she simply shook the dust from it and ran angrily on.

'Give it back!'

'Got to catch me first!' he called behind him.

They soon grew tired and stopped beneath a large old tree. She leaned against it, grateful for the wide, leafy shade of its foliage. The boy smiled and offered her the clip.

'It looks nice in your hair,' he mumbled bashfully.

Despite her anger, a great wave of happiness engulfed her. She didn't know why, nor did she understand the childish emotions making her heart pound wildly as she struggled to catch her breath. Then suddenly her brother was before them, throwing a wild punch at the boy who immediately threw one back. He had appeared as though from nowhere on the sandy path where they were standing beneath the tree. He punched the boy again. She began to cry and he grabbed her by the arm and dragged her home. On the way he called her a 'hussy', a word she did not understand.

They reached home and her brother went straight to their parents.

'She was with the boy from next door.'

The words struck like lightning bolts. Her father gave her a slap across the cheek that she would remember for the rest of her life. Her mother grabbed a handful of her hair and dragged her away.

'I'll sort her out,' she called to her husband.

'That's the last time you're going out on the streets,' she screamed at her, once they had left the room. 'No more games. You're a grown-up now, not a little girl. Go and look at yourself in the mirror. Take your sister's scarf and wrap your hair in it. I've had enough of these girls and their modern ways!'

She could still hear herself weeping, and feel her hands probing her body, searching for parts that had begun to grow, parts she had previously only known about from her mother.

But all that was in the past. Now was another time.

The walls were suffocating, constricting the cramped house. There was no refreshing breeze and the air was brutally hot. Her father was sweating.

'Where are you all?' he called to her mother. 'Aren't you dressed yet? Hurry up! It's already late and you're still getting ready.'

Her mother continued seasoning the fish while chaos reigned in the adjoining bedrooms. As usual, they had stayed up late on Thursday when her sisters and their children had arrived to spend the weekend with them.

'Stop getting in my way, both of you!' the woman yelled at the children. 'Go to your mothers and let me finish what I'm doing! And haven't you lot finished dressing and undressing yet? Will one of you please go and see your father? Ugh... these girls will be the death of me!'

Meanwhile she was alone in her bedroom, emptying the contents of her wardrobe onto the bed and trying on one piece of clothing after another. She pulled one on, examined herself then pulled it off again, already reaching for the next. Outfit after outfit and nothing seemed to suit her.

'God, I'm fed up,' she murmured to herself. 'It's so hot I feel like I'm melting. The sea looks beautiful though... If only I could chuck these stuffy clothes and have a cold bath.'

She left the room and slouched wearily to the kitchen in search of her mother.

'I've no idea what to wear, so how am I supposed to go to the beach?'

Her mother hurriedly finished what she was doing, her face shiny with sweat. Without looking at her daughter, she tied her scarf into a knot around her head.

'My head's about to explode! Go and take your anger out on someone else... and wear whatever you want to wear!'

Her frustration grew. She felt heat rise within her, even more suffocating than the surrounding air. She watched her mother with a mixture of pity and anger.

'Who am I supposed to go to? You all say the same thing. None of my sisters are free.'

'What did I just tell you? No more complaining, I'm sick of hearing about clothes. Don't ruin the day please, just behave. Moments like these don't come along very often, my dear, so don't let them slip away when they do!'

'Fine. Do you need any help?'

'No, just go and get ready.'

They all managed to squeeze onto the bus and prepared to greet the sea. They had not visited it in some time and each was hoping it would restore fond memories, and bring them an even more glorious day.

Brightly coloured kites danced through the air like little rainbows that, mingling with rays of sunshine, glowed alternately on the foam and the sand.

A strong breeze gusted through the humid air, laden with an array of scents, from sweetcorn to potatoes roasting on burning embers. It was a wonderful scene. Sizzling steam rose from carts displaying pistachios and roasted seeds, each one adorned with twinkling lights like a carnival float. And once your tongue had tired of their burning heat, another line of cheerful stalls stood in waiting, offering ice cream of all colours and flavours. How good it tasted as you strolled along the beachfront, the breeze caressing your body and the cool taste refreshing your soul!

The beach was packed with tents and small sunshades cobbled together from planks of wood, and palm fronds that wafted a cool breeze over those sitting beneath: the lovers and dreamers, yearning for a day that would steal them away from the troubles of existence. Warm light filtered through the fronds, crisscrossing the sand and filling them with hope. As the fronds swayed, bells chimed softly, tickling their ears.

Gaza's coastline is not clean. Everything is scattered about in disarray. The sand is littered with rubbish and tents dot the beach like bales of hay, where dreaming souls shelter, conversing with their most intimate imaginings. That is just the way Gaza is: a young girl yet to learn the art of elegance. A young girl who has not yet developed her own scent and is still, willingly or not, perfumed by all around her.

The family chose a tent which they soon filled with laughter, chatting happily about the day ahead. They were all in search of memories, contemplating the waves as they surged tirelessly towards the shore, awakening within them nostalgia, hope, and a sense of loss before the great cloak of the sea.

Her father did not know how to swim. He bobbed up and down in the water, relying on his height as he struggled forward before returning to the shore, where he sat contemplating the water in such profound silence that everyone knew he had drifted away to a sea far from the one before them. Their mother, meanwhile, busied herself arranging the tent, keeping an anxious eye on the salad that she had just taken from her bag, fearing it would be ruined by the sandy breeze. She was preparing their lunchtime festivities, arranging the table just as it would be at home. It was only when she sat down that she realised how tired she was. During all this, her daughter sat quietly, contemplating her parents.

Then there was Grandma, her embroidered dress fluttering in the breeze. She was chuckling away, an old cigarette balanced between her lips as she puffed out smoke and crooned melancholy folk songs of old. Every now and then, she glanced furtively at her sulky granddaughter.

'Go and have a swim, dear. I'd come with you if I could.'

'On my own?'

'Don't you have a pair of legs?'

'Yes.'

'Go on, before it gets chilly.'

'Ok, I'm going.'

Her sisters were full of laughter, winking cheekily at one another as they discussed their various acquaintances.

'God forgive us all this nattering; it's just a bit of fun!' they spontaneously declared after every round of gossip.

She smiled at her sisters' and grandmother's words, rising quietly to her feet and walking towards the sea.

Passing her brothers, who were grilling fish on the barbecue, she vaguely registered their loud discussions, alternating between politics, memories of the war and intifada, and mockery of their current situation. Vapour and ash from the hookah danced into the air along with their laughter.

None of them noticed her as she walked through the smoke. It was as though the sea had cast a spell over her, making her invisible to those around her and carrying her like a bride on her wedding day.

She passed a boy of seven, waiting for waves at the shoreline and leaping joyfully as they washed forward. He was soaked and his trousers were slipping down as he and his brother chased one another around, tossing sand and shells back and forth. Their eyes shone with the freshness of youth. They were quick to anger and quicker yet to make up and return to their game. She smiled at them, patting their heads and continuing on her way.

Another boy of four was running around naked, rejoicing in the freedom of his childhood as he flew back to his mother, anxiously awaiting his return from the water. He threw himself into her arms, seeking protection in her warmth from the secrets of the sea that his four short years had failed to comprehend.

Nearby, a group of young men were throwing cards onto the sand, each with the confident certainty of victory. They didn't have a screen to protect them from the blazing sun and their backs were already burning.

One of them twisted round to watch her as she walked past, calling out a chat-up line from where he sat, cards still in hand.

A short distance away, a donkey was immersed in the water, washing away the hardships of a day spent lugging around cartloads of people. It was laughable. Even the donkey had its own place on the beach and in the sea, splashing about in the salty water like everyone else.

Another couple of children were trying to choose which colour of Slush Puppy to dye their lips with, arguing over who would have the red and who the yellow. They were both wearing shirt and trousers and both soaked to the skin. The vendor, meanwhile, sitting behind his simple little cart, was chuckling into his thick white beard, muttering silent wishes and prayers, all swallowed up in the depths of the sea.

At another stall, a young teenager, still clinging to childhood, hurried forward to buy some lupin beans. He began to strip their skins, chucking them around him in the pervasive chaos of early teenage years. His eyes were bashful and he avoided everyone's gaze, too shy to swim with girls and longing for another sea that would carry him – and his lupin skins – off to some anonymous location. Nearby, the scents of tea and cardamom-infused coffee were wafting from hot coals as an old man recounted tales of the country's history and wars, and of friends long gone.

Behind him, two high-spirited youths were roaring up the path on a motorcycle, carried forward by blaring music and vying with the wind as it gusted in the opposite direction. Their hair was styled into what looked like miniature Eiffel Towers on top of their heads, while their minds remained firmly rooted in the Middle Ages, as they ogled and wolf-whistled at every veiled girl in sight, revelling in their virility. But a towering policeman soon went to block their path, and the motorcycle squealed to a halt, the young men tumbling to the ground and their protests fading amidst the girls' laughter.

'Leave them be. They're happy!' a passer-by smiled to the policeman, walking around the prostrate figures.

The flirtatious attentions of young men on the beach varied from the original and witty to the downright harassing but, in spite of their rowdiness, they added to the warm, festive atmosphere, delighting in all those around them.

But she was oblivious to the surrounding bustle, pursuing her elusive memories as they led towards the sea. The noise of the past would grant her no respite. Her black dress rustled in the breeze and her headscarf fluttered a greeting to the seagulls. With every step that carried her closer to the water, she heard what sounded like the neighing of horses, growing steadily louder inside her.

She drifted forward, carried like a mermaid by the breeze, her thoughts entirely immersed in the waves before her. Time was stealing her steps away, and the sea, without her realising, had already snuck into her memory.

Between the fragrant scent of nostalgia and that of the sea, memories crashed together in her mind as waves surged towards her. She felt the sting of sand biting at her soft skin and longed to escape the black folds of her dress. She sunk her toes into the wet sand, her footprints as light as a butterfly's, dissolving instantly away. She moved forward, fearful of what was to come. Her foot had plunged into an abyss too deep to escape. But she continued, happy to have fallen. Her ivory feet were now soaked and golden grains of sand glistened around them.

She swam further out. Water seeped beneath her clothes until they ballooned around her. She felt an excited tingle that was almost too much to bear. Arousal grew inside her as she continued onwards, oblivious to the seashells cutting the bottom of her feet, making the moment complete with a few drops of female blood. Pain and desire gripped her. Sea foam surrounded her like a bracelet of honey, entwined with froths of whipped candyfloss, its edges gleaming with golden light as it absorbed its nectar from the sun above.

Gazing up at the brilliant white of the sky, she was carried along like an angel of the sea. The cold sea breeze whipped at her skin, sharper even than the biting sand. With eyes shut, she took a deep breath and plunged beneath a wave. It had barely run its course when she already felt an urgent need for air. She surged upwards and her dress billowed out. Tugging it hastily down, she gasped for breath and blushed as she saw the black material clinging to her breasts, displaying her curves to anyone who cared to look.

Her cheeks glowed and her dark eyes shone like precious stones, fringed by eyelashes as sharp as arrows. Rays of sun bathed her in a halo of light and her smile filled the shore with boundless joy. She felt air rushing from her and realised she was panting, struggling to catch a single breath.

'I want to keep swimming,' she murmured to herself. 'I want to fly beneath the waves. I want to be as light as a feather on water.'

The sea's symphony, familiar and divine, caressed her ears. Her heart slowed and reached out to the desolate expanse of water. She opened her eyes and was dazzled by golden ripples stretching out as far as she could see. Her body sunk into their warm embrace.

She swam further, propelling herself forward with slender arms and legs as her dress swirled around her, entangling her thighs and restricting their movement. Her scarf, meanwhile, had plastered her hair to her head and felt as though it had been fastened there permanently, covering her eyes.

Her feet no longer touched the ground and she grew afraid, pulling the scarf from her face and turning to look behind her. The people on the beach were tiny dots in the distance and she could barely distinguish them. They too must no longer be able to see her. A strong current was pulling her dress down and she shivered in alarm, sensing her strength fade and fearing she could no longer stay afloat. Her legs felt heavy with the material wrapped tightly around them and she wanted to pull it off but was afraid of her nakedness. She was afraid of death too, and of shame. She loved life and felt suddenly alone. The sky was far above and the sea had grown menacing, its echoing boom resounding in her ears. Tears would not come although she desperately wanted to cry. She gave in to the current but, as she began to go under, a muscular arm suddenly encircled her. She gazed down at it, feeling its strength and warmth.

'I've got you. Hold tight and don't be afraid.'

She grew even more alarmed as scenes from the past flashed before her, urging her to keep far away from any man she did not know. Faint voices rose from the depths. Her mother and father's scolding tones filled her ears. It was her first day of secondary school again, as she proudly stepped out in her new uniform: a child realising she had grown up for the first time, aware of her girlish curves beneath the material and sensing her hair waving in the breeze. Everyone on the street had watched her with an admiration she had not fully comprehended. But she had, at least, understood that she was attractive, and in full possession of herself. Next, she saw a young boy of her own age. He smiled at her and she felt herself smile back. Then there was a path shaded by branches. She and the boy were sheltering beneath a tree as the boy told her how beautiful she was and she felt as though all the birds in the trees were singing for her and her alone. All she could recall was his smile and his broken tooth, both of which she had immediately loved and would never forget. The rest of his features were hazy, fading to nothing as her brother appeared before them, punching the boy and dragging her away by the arm. Then she woke from her reverie, feeling her rescuer tug harder on her arm. They were approaching the shore. She moved feebly and was barely able to draw breath, but she was afraid of him coming any closer. And yet she had liked his arm gripped tightly around her. It gave her a feeling of security she thought she had lost many years ago.

Sunlight dazzled her as she opened her eyes. Tears fell onto her cheeks and lay glistening there. She felt incapable of coherent speech.

'Let me go, I'll carry on by myself.' Garbled words escaped her: 'What will people say?'

The young man smiled in surprise, swimming strongly forward.

'They'll say "look at that handsome young man who's rescued that gorgeous girl."'

'What do you know? Maybe I wanted to die,' she said, overwhelmed by exhaustion.

'No. You got a taste of death so you'd learn to appreciate life. Next time, I'll teach you to swim.'

They lingered in the water, now safe from harm. She glanced into his eyes.

'How?'

'Maybe it was me who was going to give up on life until I saw your eyes,' he said, his words interrupted by the waves washing over them.

They walked the rest of the way to the beach. One of her brothers, a year younger than her, was watching them. In his face, she saw confusion and anger, mingled with affection.

'What happened? Are you OK?' he called, coming towards them.

She remained silent, staring at him wordlessly as she drifted in and out of a daze. The man replied instead.

'She was drowning. But she's fine now, thank God.'

Her brother stepped forward, took his hand, and shook it vigorously.

She remained standing between them. The young man smiled, leaning down to whisper in her ear.

'Didn't I tell you? Life's simpler than you think.'

She gazed at his familiar smile and broken tooth. She remembered her hairclip, the walls of the neighbours' house and the shade of the tree, then felt her heart take flight once more.

She longed for a childhood that had faded away amidst the scolding severity of her family, suddenly afraid of their neighbourhood's scorn.

Black Grapes

Early Afternoon

AN OLD MAN CAN be seen leaning on a fence stake with a mobile phone in his hand. There isn't any room on his face for a smile; the furrows on his brow whorl around a deep centre, like the eye of a storm, a hole in time. Leaning over an unplastered wall, he plucks a grape from a vine and grinds it between his teeth. It makes a satisfying squelch. He takes another, inspects its size, glossy and black between his fingers. The sunlight bounces off its surface as he turns it, as he hears a breeze rustling the vines on the hill behind him. It is the middle of August and the heat is already brutal. He licks the sticky juice from his fingers, sucking each finger loudly, then makes the call: 'Hello, Bitahon?[1] There appears to be a terrorist in the Efrat settlement.'

Within a couple of minutes, security guards in flak jackets swarm into the street, followed by fully armed soldiers. A house at the end of the row becomes surrounded, and a 40-year-old man can be seen coming to the front window brandishing a hunting rifle, screaming. They shoot him in the head, then break down the door, and from all the shouting it's clear another man has been found. As he's dragged out, past the body of the dead man in the front room, it's evident he's distressed. By the time they get him outside, his shirt is covered in the other man's blood. 'What have you done? He didn't do anything! I didn't pay him!' he screams. 'I didn't pay him…'

In a student bar, on the campus of Bar-Ilan University in Tel Aviv, a 19-year-old economics undergraduate becomes distracted from his drink. On the TV screen above the bartender, an old man can be seen repeating the same plaintive phrase: 'I didn't pay him!' It's his father. The 'Breaking News' feed along the bottom of the screen reads: 'Settler killed in Efrat: Terrorist believed to have entered through perimeter fence.'

The student cannot understand what's going on. He stares at his drink vacantly, and mumbles to himself: 'When are they going to understand?'

The Night Before

In the last light of dusk, an old woman, whose face is riven with wrinkles, can be seen trudging along the rugged mountain road between al-Khader village and the Efrat settlement. She wears an embroidered dress and a white handkerchief tied around her head. It is four miles from her home to the vines she owns near the settlement. She walks alongside a donkey pulling a cart full of water barrels to irrigate the vines. Her oldest son passes her, with another donkey and cart, this time laden with grapes, going in the opposite direction. Without even trying to make out his face in the growing darkness, she knows it's him.

'Hammoud, what are you doing here, and so late?' she asks.

'I have to take these to Bethlehem,' he replies gesturing at the grapes. 'The shorter route has too much security on our side.'

'Grapes? You son of a...,' she yells at him. 'Where did you get them? I can see they're not ours!'

'Don't ask, Mama.'

'Don't shame me, more like! Your father was prepared to be run over by a bulldozer before he gave up his grapes. And now you do this. I curse the very bitch that bore you,' she spits in his face.

They set off again in opposite directions.

As she approaches her land, she is greeted by the still-unfamiliar lights of the settlements that surround it on all sides. The smell of the soil triggers a cascade of memories, wrapped up with the soft dew that is even now beginning to settle on the leaves. She ties the donkey's reigns to a tree and with her sprinkler-hose starts to water the vines. As she does so, she examines each tree's clusters of small, unhealthy-looking grapes, picking out the ripe ones, and throwing them onto a sheet of cloth she's spread across the ground. She will leave these here to turn into raisins, as they are too heavy for her to carry.

Meanwhile, Hammoud gets a good price for his grapes from one of the big traders at the Bethlehem market. With the money in his pocket, he sets off immediately back to Efrat, determined to be home by early morning.

17

Early Hours of the Morning

As the rising sun dapples the ground under the orchards' boughs, a 40-year-old man sits eating breakfast with another, in his mid-sixties. The trees are laden with all kinds of fruit: grapes, figs, peaches, apples, quinces. The smell of every flavour fills the air. They talk all through their breakfast. The older man tells the younger one: 'The miracle of Efrat is that it is surrounded by five hills, all of which are named after the bounties they provide: Rimon, Gefen, Dekel, Zayit and Dagan.[2] Paradise on earth.'

'I have a favour to ask, my friend,' the younger man interjects. 'Leave my mother's land out of your plans.'

'Convince her to sell to us.'

'She refuses; it's all she has left of my father. It's too personal for her.'

'I'll talk to someone,' the older man reassures him. 'Don't worry, we'll sort something out.'

'I won't forget this favour,' Hammoud smiles. 'Do you know what my mother sings when she picks the grapes?'

'What?'

'"*The sweetness of the grapes of Alkhalil,*
the waters of Salsabil,
is the legacy of generation after generation,
and a long history of struggle."'[3]

The older man laughs and pats his companion on the shoulder. 'By the sound of it, she really *isn't* going to sell us that land...'

As they eat, a third man approaches them.

'David, have you lost your mind?' he shouts out. 'What the hell are you doing? Eating with a labourer... Just look at the Arab's hands, he's filthy!'

David stands up. 'How dare you speak that way... Apologise at once, you vile elitist!' They exchange insults for a moment; the newcomer accusing David of offending his forefathers' most sacred beliefs. Then David picks up his hunting rifle and swings it at him, instructing the newcomer very slowly to kindly get off his property.

As they watch the man retreat, Hammoud thanks David, who seems out of breath from the confrontation. They finish their food, then Hammoud starts his day's work. He trims the grass around David's house, prunes the hedge around the garden, and picks more grapes along with the other workers. He has seniority so he supervises the other labourers.

In the afternoon, Hammoud asks David for his bonus.

'I don't have it right now,' David explains.

'But I told you I needed it urgently. My children will go hungry this week without it.'

'Not my problem. Your only guaranteed salary is your cut from the grapes. You've taken more than your allowance of grapes this month.'

'Everything I sold I paid back to you, minus my seller's fee. What I'm talking about is my payment for working your land,' Hammoud starts to raise his voice.

'Again, not my problem.'

'It's your problem because I work for you.'

'You agreed the terms of your contract when you started. The gardening bonus is discretionary, you knew that. Why did you sign up if it was such a bad deal?'

'I needed the money to help my mother plant more on her own land. And now my son needs tuition fees for his first semester in college.'

'Well, my son is studying at Bar-Ilan University, and he

needs a lot *more* money,' David laughs. 'So I don't have a bonus for you this week, I'm afraid.'

'It's not for this week; it's for the last four weeks, old man.'

David decides he doesn't care for this conversation anymore and takes another sip of his coffee. Leaning back in his bamboo chair he announces: 'I'm bored now, Hammoud. Get back to work. Prattling won't get you any more grapes for the market!'

Hammoud's fury grows. He charges at the old man, lifting him up over his shoulder, and carrying him into the house. Inside, he drops him to the floor and picks up the old man's rifle. 'What are you doing, you crazy Arab?' David yells at him. Then: 'Help! Help!'

'Not before you give me my money,' Hammoud replies, pointing the rifle at him. 'I'm going to sit here and drink your coffee,' Hammoud pulls over a chair and sits in it. 'It's very comfortable this chair of yours. Go on, old man. Go and find the money you owe me.'

David shouts his reply loud enough for everyone on the street to hear. 'I'm not giving you any money, you fucking terrorist.'

The man David had kicked off his land that morning happens to be lurking, at that precise moment, by an unplastered wall on the opposite side of the street. As the afternoon sun turns its back on the vines, he leans on a fence stake and licks the juice of a grape he'd pinched from David's land from his fingers. He takes out his phone and punches in a familiar number. The sound of the grape squelching in his mouth mixes with the sounds of the crickets. 'Bitahon? There appears to be a terrorist in the Efrat settlement.'

Notes

1.   Bitahon – Hebrew word for 'security', also used to mean settlement security services specifically.

2.   Rimon – pomegranates, Gefen – grapevine, Dekel – date palm, Zayit – olive, Dagan – grain.

3.   A Palestinian song from the 1960s, titled 'The Grapes of Alkhalil' (or 'The Grapes of Hebron'), based on a poem by Ezz El-Din El-Manasra, set to music by composer Hussein Nazek.

The Mirror

As soon as she finishes her lunch, she runs to her grandmother's room. The scent of musk clings to the bedroom walls. Climbing onto the old wooden bed, she props a pillow behind her back, stretches her short legs out in front of her, then crosses one over the other, the way she has seen her grandmother do. On the wall facing the bed hangs a mirror in a thick wooden frame. A keychain – her grandfather's car keys – is pulled out of her dress pocket, and set down on the quilt beside her. She takes a long, stern look at herself in the mirror, all the time combing her fringe with her fingers. Then she shouts: 'Aunty Luuu-la, I'm waiting!'

'I'm coming, Dahlia, I'm coming,' Leila replies from the hallway, but her niece won't relent.

'Here,' the girl says as Leila finally enters the room. 'Sit next to me. Put a pillow behind your back like I did.' She pats her grandfather's pillow, and Leila leans over to place a kiss on the little girl's forehead. As she lowers herself on to the bed, a single strand of Leila's hair catches the light and shines like silver thread.

'Right, I'm here. Reporting for duty. What are my orders?'

The girl looks at her aunt in the mirror, carefully following her movements. Leila catches the girl's eye in the mirror, and smiles. At this, Dahlia picks up the car keys, points the plastic fob at the mirror, and presses the remote locking button, declaring: 'Aunty Luuu-la, let's watch TV. It's time for *Masha!*'

Leila has to stop herself from laughing, seeing how serious her niece is. 'Oh wow, Masha! Of course, let's watch it together,' she says, remembering the girl's favourite cartoon. Dahlia giggles at the attention her aunt is now paying to the game, then goes back to pushing the button on the fob. A little red light at the end of the fob flashes with each press.

'Oh, are we changing channel now? Not too fast, we need to see what's on each one,' warns Leila.

'No, I'm just trying to find the one with the best signal,' Dahlia explains.

'Okay, keep looking then.'

Leila watches her niece. She wants to hug her, she's so proud of her, but would never interrupt a game she took so seriously.

'Luuu-la, look, it's Masha!' Dahlia suddenly exclaims.

'Oh, yes. There she is. Look at her golden fringe peeking out from under her little white scarf!'

As her niece goes on to describe what she imagines somewhere beyond her reflection in the mirror, Leila can't take her eyes off the ingenious three-year-old personality sitting beside her. 'Aunty, look! Masha is drowning in the sea!' She points suddenly to the window, to where the real, pale blue sea of Gaza can be seen. 'The bear has jumped into the sea to save her!' she continues, then pretends to be the bear, outstretching her arms, growling and throwing herself around the bed. Eventually, she sits up and wipes imaginary water from her face, taking turns to look at the mirror and then her aunt.

With rushed, half-pronounced words, and a face more animated than any cartoon character, Dahlia tells Leila the full story of today's episode. Alongside the basic plot, she also offers a side commentary about her own fear of water, something her aunt is all too familiar with.

For a second, Leila imagines herself drowning in the waters of the mirror. She remembers another little girl, perfectly drawn, her blonde hair in buns that danced against the sky like puffy clouds. Her name was 'Laidy', and Leila sees her now, chasing the sunset in the opening credits, running across a meadow towards a horizon where the grass is shoulder-high. But Dahlia's screams bring her back to the present.

'Oh, Aunty. Masha drowned! The bear couldn't save her.' A look of dejection has spread across her niece's face.

'Don't be afraid, habeebti, he can still save her,' Leila says.

But just as quickly, Leila retreats back to the mirror. She sees a dark staircase, and small feet striding upwards, jumping one step at a time, like a rabbit. Her nursery school teacher told her about rabbits, and she thinks of them now as she climbs the stairs. Despite the darkness, she bravely climbs up and up, shining an imaginary torch ahead of her, until the moment she's grabbed from behind by a pair of unseen hands. Hands that start to run all over her body. The body of a four-year-old at a turn in the stairs of her own life. The imaginary torch goes out. She doesn't know what these hands are trying to do. Are they feeling for a pattern, a drawing of a treasure map, perhaps? Her nanny once told her the story of a sea captain who drew a treasure map on his arm to hide it from others. But she doesn't know what these hands are doing, or why they are removing her underwear. What drawing can there possibly be down there?

'Aunty, Masha's screaming!' Dahlia interrupts. 'She wants the bear to help her.'

But Leila has swum out too far now, where shells and coloured stones glimmer on the sea floor beneath her. 'Don't worry, he *will* help her,' she reassures. 'Look how big and strong he is: he loves her like I love you.'

There is a tear in Leila's abdomen, as a hand reaches round to cover her mouth. She feels as if her legs have been trapped in blocks of ice. Only a few steps separate her from her family's front door on the first floor. But it is dark. The hands move away: 'Where is your house?'

The girl points a trembling hand to the door: 'There.'

'Stand here. Don't move. I'll be back in a minute to check you haven't moved.'

Dahlia bangs on the headboard to get her aunt's attention: 'Aunty Luuu-la, he's saving her! Masha's not going to die.'

She knocks on the door. She screams. But her fists are too small and the wood of the door too thick for her to be heard. She screams and screams until her voice is hoarse and her throat stings. Suddenly a neighbour across the hall opens her door and sees the girl, with tears streaming down her face. She rings the doorbell that the girl hadn't been able to reach. A woman opens the door and is instantly horrified. 'My daughter, what's wrong? Where have you been? We've been worried sick.' The girl doesn't answer. Tears continue to stream down her face.

Her teenage cousin comes to the door as well, mirroring her mother's worried expression. 'Leila, are you alright?'

'She's got a pack of cigarettes in her hand!' her mother exclaims.

The girl's cousin looks at her in shame: 'I sent her out to buy me some. She was jumping up and down at the window wanting to get out. She asked if she could buy me anything, like a pack of cigarettes, so I let her go. I'm so sorry.'

The mother carries the girl to her bed, the neighbour and her cousin follow. 'Did anyone approach you?' her mother asks. 'What happened?'

'Masha's not going to die!'

Leila hugs her little niece, and notices for the first time that she's coughing. Feeling the girl's forehead and cheeks, she can sense a fever coming on, and remembers her reply to her mother's question: 'He was a thief. He wanted to take me away. He said he was coming back. Maybe he went to get a knife, to kill me. He went up the stairs.'

Without a second's thought, the mother picks her up and marches out of the apartment and up the stairs, taking two steps at a time. The others follow her, panting and struggling to keep up. 'Where are you, you son of a bitch?' she bellows as she makes her way up towards the construction workshop on the top floor.

The building was an unfinished, four-storey affair, typical of many on Mishum Amer Street, in the 'Black Rock' quarter of Yarmouk.[1] This whole neighbourhood had been flooded recently by new arrivals – displaced Syrians from the Golan Heights and Quneitra,[2] Palestinians from Black September,[3] not to mention Kurds and Circassians – so it was common for people to live on the lower floors of half-built buildings with stairwells that hadn't been fully wired up yet.

'Take a good look at their faces, my girl. Which one of them did it?' the mother shouts as they march into the workshop.

The girl inspects each one of them men carefully. It had been dark when it happened, and she hadn't seen his face, only his hands and a flash of white shirt. He seemed tall, that is all she can tell her mother... which isn't enough.

Failing to identify any one culprit, they retreat back to their apartment on the first floor. The father is away with work. The girl cries all night, and develops a temperature. When she wakes in the morning, a single strand of white hair has appeared in her fringe. On seeing it, her cousin bursts into sobs: 'Oh habeebti, they were my cigarettes. It's all my fault. Forgive me. Please forgive me!'

The car's headlights are the first thing she remembers of what happened, followed by the sound of her own panting as she ran round the front of the building from the lobby to the grocer's that took up the rest of the ground floor. She remembers thinking that someone on the other side of the street was standing unusually still. Despite the distance, she knew he was looking at her. She remembers jeans. He wore jeans. When the light from the passing car turned from her to him, she dared to look straight at him. But it moved away too quickly. So she didn't see his face. It was him, though.

She remains afraid of that staircase her entire life. She has nightmares for many years about the shadow that can make hands appear out of nowhere, grabbing her. But she always kept Laidy close: Laidy who runs though green orchards.

She remains Leila's favourite cartoon character, even into adulthood. In nightmares, she too runs for the comfort of those green meadows, keeping the sunlight on her face rather than darkness.

She takes the car keys out of Dahlia's chubby fingers: 'Let's change the channel, shall we? Look, Dahlia. Masha's climbing a mountain!'

Dahlia jumps like a rabbit, her feet planted wide apart in the bedspread. She jumps again, laughing. Her eyes sparkle and her little teeth glint like pearls. 'The rabbit's going to jump up high, like me,' she says.

'Yes,' Leila says. 'Sky high.'

Notes

1.   Yamouk – a Palestinian refugee camp in the Syrian capital, Damascus.

2.   Quneitra – the largely destroyed and abandoned capital of the Quneitra Governorate in south-western Syria. Situated in a high valley in the strategically important Golan Heights, it was captured by Israel in the last day of the 1967 Six Day War, before being briefly retaken by Syria during the 1973 Yom Kippur War, then recaptured again by Israel in a subsequent counter-offensive. Since 1974, pursuant to UN Security Council Resolution 350, it has been classed as inside the UN-patrolled 'buffer zone'.

3.   Black September – a conflict fought in Jordan between the Jordanian Armed Forces, under the leadership of King Hussein, and the PLO (Palestine Liberation Organisation), under the leadership of Yasser Arafat, primarily between 16 and 27 September 1970.

Pen and Notebook

THEIR FEET WERE TOO small for the task. They lengthened their strides as the road opened up before them, breaking into a run, panting, filling their tiny lungs with the excitement of being out of school. Tattered shoes pounded the tarmac, fringed by the frayed edges of school trousers. Old schoolbags bounced up and down their backs. On either side of them lay the rubble of destroyed buildings, like the damage caused by a storm that had torn through the little city overnight.

The sky was getting lighter as the sun inched upwards.

A donkey-pulled cart waited for them at the end of the street. Jumping into it, the two boys were greeted by their older brother's usual complaints: 'I told you a million times, you need to get here sooner. I am tired of always waiting for you. We're losing valuable time here.' They could hardly see the older brother's face under his baseball cap; his skin was so dark from endless days spent in the burning sun that only the whites of his eyes could be seen under its brim.

'Giddy-up!' he cried, with a crack of his whip, and the cart jolted into motion.

The donkey was no show pony; there was nothing graceful about the way it trotted down the road. Every pot-hole bounced its passengers into the air, and the sound of its metal shoes scraping the tarmac was painful. But it was a hard worker, and patient, as were the three boys it lugged around all day. The cart took up more of the road than was allowed, often jutting out into the pavement. Together, the donkey, cart and boys didn't abide by the city's traffic laws; they constituted a rogue body, following its own rules, only caring that it reached its destination, with all components still intact.

'Get off the road!' shouted one driver. 'Are you mad?'

'The road is for cars,' added a policeman, loitering on a street corner.

The fifteen-year-old at the reins ignored them, pulling down his cap till it covered his eyes; 'Giddy-up, Donkey,' he repeated, along with those encouraging clicking sounds donkeys appreciate if you want them to obey you. Twenty minutes later they were there.

The children threw down their bags and disembarked into what might have looked like a warren of sand dunes rising and falling ahead of them, had it not been made of fractured concrete and twisted metal.

Adham, the youngest of the three boys, quickly scrambled to the top of the nearest heap, and began picking out small rocks to pass to his brother, Asaad, who took up position a few paces below him on the side of the heap. Instead of handing them down to him, however, Adham had learned to throw them with such precision and care that they always landed gently and perfectly in Asaad's hands. The boy at the top of the heap had an eye like a telescope; he could not only find the right sized stones instantly, but could judge throwing distances down to the last millimetre. He analysed everything from his vantage point, the way a surveyor measures a circle of land from every position.

It was getting hotter. Bulldozers and stone-crushers were appearing all around them; huge machines whose first job was to clear a space on the ground from which to work. One set of vehicles was having to start the day by clearing a building that had actually been destroyed in a previous war, as it was blocking the way to more recent devastation. Adham worked hard, picking out stones with speed and efficiency, and throwing them to Asaad without even looking up as he did so. He knew the size and weight of each stone at first glance – a skill he had perfected through months of practice. Having not long established a momentum, with his brother completing the chain down to the cart beneath them, something red suddenly caught Adham's eye in among the rubble. A toy truck. He stared at it. *If we had a real truck*, he thought, *we'd be able to put a whole day's stones in it, and not have to go backwards and forwards all day with that rickety old cart.*

For a moment, the boy forgot where he was and began playing with it among the concrete fragments. He smiled as he pushed it along the jamb of a door, now horizontal, then shook himself and stuffed it into his pocket. 'What are you doing?' Asaad was shouting. 'I'm waiting here. Did you forget about me?' His voice could hardly be made out against the noise of the bulldozers. The youngest boy cupped his hands around his ear to catch the words. 'No, I didn't forget,' he shouted back. 'I'll explain later.'

Ayham, the eldest boy, was further afield gathering his own rocks – much larger than the ones being thrown about by his brothers. These were heavy, square chunks of dolomite, used in the older houses or as cladding in the best new builds; great white bricks carved from the quarries of the West Bank. Carrying them hurt his back and left his hands scratched and swollen, but he was getting stronger every day. He felt this. As he worked, he noticed a girl about his age dressed in a blue galabia and a backpack walking towards him from a distance. Each time he set a new stone down on the cart, he looked up at her, surreptitiously, wondering at her smooth, pale skin. But he felt himself blushing as he did so, and tried to work out why he was so embarrassed as he walked back to the heap.

The stones filled up the cart in three distinct piles: the large square blocks Ayham brought, plus two other piles – one of medium-sized rocks, maybe the size of an adult's hand, the other small enough to fit in a schoolboy's fist. As Asaad caught the stones thrown down to him, he would quickly decide which of these two piles he should throw them onto. As he did so, he couldn't help thinking of the three piles – small, medium and large – as somehow representing the three brothers.

Against Ayham's slow, steady progress to and from the cart, the younger boys seemed to be almost playing. Stones flew between them as lightly as their laughter, with each boy speeding up every so often to see if the other could keep up. Behind their silhouettes, Ayham could see the sun beginning to set; its flaming rays had gathered together and found a new order, just as the stones had found a new arrangement in the back of their cart. Deciding the cart was full, Ayham called his brothers down from their heap. The boys clambered down happily, as Ayham pulled out a large bed sheet from underneath a piece of plaster board. Without a second thought for its original owner, he stretched the sheet carefully over the contents of the cart, securing it to all four sides. Once again, the three boys threw on their backpacks; the youngest, Adham, smiling to himself at the thought of the toy truck now stowed safely in his.

'Giddy-up, Donkey,' the oldest boy shouted, as the other two giggled and mimicked him, mustering all the pleasure of a *fellah* heading back from the fields after a long day's work.

The boy's beaming smiles infected passers-by. The younger boys, Asaad and little Adham were pleased with what they'd accomplished, despite the lacework of scratches and scars that covered their soft palms and the tears in their clothes. Only the donkey felt unhappy; it strained against the weight of the rocks the boys had collected. The traffic was heavy, and the cart had to make many stops and starts. Each time it did, smaller stones, having spilled down their pile, kept rolling off the cart from under the sheet. At one point a whole bunch of stones fell out at once, forcing Adham to stop the cart, and his two brothers to jump out and pick them up again. The cars' honking behind them escalated, drivers' voices grew angrier. Even pedestrians shouted at them.

'Do you have a death wish, kid?' One driver shouted, slapping the side of his door. 'I could barely see you down there. I could have driven over you! What the hell are your parents doing, leaving you to crawl around in the road all day?'

The two boys barely noticed the shouting. Their eyes were glued to the tarmac, scanning in all directions to see where the stones had scattered. A few minutes later they were back on the cart and moving.

'Hey, boy,' shouted a policeman pulling up alongside them on a motorbike. 'Dismount this thing and take it off the road, now. I'm issuing you with a ticket.' Ayham just looked at the policeman, then stared forward at the road again, in silence. The cart carried on. At this, the officer pulled out in front of them, then slowed his bike down, ushering the cart diagonally to the side of the road.

'Please, sir. Let me go on my way. People are waiting for us at home. They'll be worried.'

'You're too young to be operating a vehicle on the street. And you don't seem to be aware of the chaos being caused by all the rubbish you're dropping.'

'Please, sir,' this time it was Adham, reaching into his backpack with a sombre face, in the cart behind. 'You can have it back. I won't do it again, I promise.'

For a moment the officer wasn't sure what he was looking at: a plastic red truck, with shiny black wheels and a white cabin, was being held out to him by a child who couldn't be more than seven years old. The man laughed. 'Keep it,' he waved. 'Keep it.' And before he could gather himself from whatever memory the toy had triggered, the cart was half way up the street.

This time the traffic was clear and the cart began to pick up speed. The donkey was tired but it seemed to understand that they were late. As they sped along, the four of them were a spectacle to behold: donkey and children ghoulishly white, covered as they were in the fine white dust of the rubble; rocks rolling and bouncing in the back in a constant low cacophony. The younger boys, sitting in the back, tried to weather the bumps in the road as best they could; but, each time, their starts of pain and cries of discomfort quickly turned to laughter: a running joke between them was which one of them had the biggest bottom, most able to take the constant prodding and jolting of the rocks beneath them.

As they approached Rimal Street, they spotted a brightly coloured cart parked on the pavement, selling biscuits. An old man, presumably the proprietor, stood behind, as a child no more than five of six years old patrolled in front, calling out, 'Biscuits! Biscuits! Biscuits!' to passing traffic. The boys couldn't help themselves. With one dirty shekel fished from the bottom of Ayham's backpack, they bought a single biscuit. They split it three ways and began nibbling at each piece, savouring its crumbly pleasure as if this were the most expensive biscuit in the world. The scent and softness of the biscuit's flour seemed to mingle with the dust of their fingers.

By 5:30pm, the cart had arrived at its destination in the northwest corner of the city, and the three children leapt to the task of unloading the stones. They were paid for their day's work by a merchant who surveyed the various piles of material that arrived each day. Twenty-four shekels was handed over in return for the stones. Ayham, taking the money from the hands of this grumpy, burly man, made sure not to look him in the eye; a shudder of happiness passed through him, as he gazed at the note and coins in his hands, but it was quickly replaced by a worry: would this be enough to last to the same time tomorrow evening? But then he dismissed this thought too: *God provides*, as his mother always said.

Finally it was time for the three boys, their wooden cart, their tired donkey, and Adham's newly acquired shiny red truck to head home. Now empty, their little cart crossed the centre of the devastated city, passing half-toppled residential blocks, office buildings pouring out smoke into the night sky, several completely new gaps in the city's architecture where entire buildings had been flattened.

The boys arrived into Shuja'aya with yells and whistles, their voices echoing through the camp, bouncing off the tin walls of the huts and caravans that had been their neighbours' homes since the last war drove them out of their farmlands. The cart stopped.

As they ran into their trailer, birds scattered from the hot tin roof above them. Their father lay on his bed, drenched in sweat, barely able to move, as was his fate since an American-made bullet had cut through his spine eight years before. The children planted three gentle kisses on his forehead before going to clean up. The dust still clinging to their faces left white smudges on his skin. Their mother, Om Ayham, sat beside him. By the light of a small candle, she sewed together dresses from a strips of material stacked beside her. Her eyes were tired. Time had left deep etches on her once soft face. The work needed to be completed if she was to be paid in the morning. Returning from the sink, clean and refreshed, the children surrounded their mother hugging her from three sides.

The warmth of her body seemed to restore them from the chill that had crept in since that evening's sun had set. Ayham withdrew the crumpled 20 shekel note from his trouser pocket, and placed it in his mother's hand. Her eyes glistened and he gave her a kiss on the forehead. Of the four shekels that remained, he gave two each to his brothers. 'Don't forget what I told you. Buy a notebook and a pen so you can learn to write like me,' he said in his most paternal voice.

White Lilies

21 March 1997
Tel Aviv

A YOUNG MAN IS running along J. L. Gordon Street. With his thin, delicate features, and chestnut hair blowing in the breeze, he catches the eye of everyone he passes. It is still early when he arrives at 98 Ben Yehuda Street, the florists with the green-lettered sign: *GORDON FLOWERS*. As the door clatters behind him he gasps for air, and leans on the counter for a moment to catch his breath. The young shop assistant smiles at him, surrounded by a jungle of white lilies. His grin emphasises a deep dimple in his left cheek, while his hair looks jet black against all the white.

'So, you're a jogger?' the shop assistant asks.

'I'm new here,' replies the young man. 'I've been trying to see as much of the place as possible – It's beautiful.'

'Where were you before?'

'France.'

'Ah! I bet the flowers there are wonderful.'

'They certainly are,' the young man chuckles, then finally straightens up. 'Erm... I'd like some flowers for my mother, for Mother's Day.'

'Lilies are the flower for this occasion,' says the shop assistant. 'White ones, as you can see.'

'You're the expert.'

The man with the dimple laughs: 'A cup of coffee and a bouquet of white lilies – the perfect present!'

'And a croissant!' the young man adds in his thick french accent.

The two young men exchange money and shake hands, smiling, and for a moment all the differences between them disappear.

Gaza Beach

It is nearing midnight when the man with a dimple in his left cheek arrives at his home in al-Shatea Camp – a bouquet of white lilies in his hand. The smell of the sea lingers in the sandy streets, where houses crowd together either side of alleyways too narrow for even a donkey cart to pass through. These are simple houses, made from sheets of corrugated asbestos, echoing with the sound of the seagulls splashing in the sea. Just as he arrives, the door of the house opposite opens and his neighbour steps out, smiling broadly: 'Ali, there you are. I have great news! I have a daughter.'

Through sleepy eyes, Ali gives the man an affectionate look. 'So, you're a father now?' He grasps him by the palm and gives him the bouquet of white lilies. 'Have you thought about the name Zahra?' Ali asks.

'Zahra it is!' The new father replies, making the orphaned seventeen-year-old very happy.

21 March 2008[1]
Gaza City

Without taking her eyes off the sky, she plaits her thick hair into two braids, then sits back at a desk by an open window, trying to focus on her homework. The house is quiet except for a persistent buzzing noise. Her mother is at work and her father sits at the table preparing for the afternoon shift; the classes at school are divided into shifts as well. Zahra is getting restless as she sits cross-legged on her chair.

'Baba, the sound of the mosquito is hurting my ears,' she shouts into the next room. 'How can something so small fill the whole house with its racket?' Her father smiles to himself and goes in to give her a hug.

'My naughty one. You're just looking for an excuse for me to do your homework for you.'

'I'm not, Baba. It's annoying!'

'How about we close all the windows,' he suggests, then watches as she jumps up off her chair, picks it up, and carries it to the each window in turn. One by one, she slams the windows shut, clambering onto her chair to reach them.

'That's better isn't it?' he says when she returns.

'Baba, the girls at school were talking about a big mosquito that launches rockets from the sky.'

'No, no, sweetheart,' he replies. 'There's no such thing.'

The girl inspects her father's face, 'Then tell me, what is that noise?'

'It's a mosquito, but it doesn't launch any rockets. You can be sure of that... The sky only sends us rain and flowers, doesn't it?'

'Yes, Baba. And the insects help the flowers grow as well, don't they? My teacher told us about them; she had a special word for them: "drones". They're not really mosquitos at all; they're much bigger – like airplanes but with no pilot. They spray pesticides from the sky. I want to be a drone operator when I grow up. I want to spray the fields so the flowers and trees can grow quickly. Imagine seeing all those green spaces on my computer screen! 'Buzzzz, buzzzz – look Baba, I'm a mosquito.'

Her father laughs as she runs around the room flapping her arms, but a darkness sits behind his eyes.

'Can I be a drone operator when I'm older, Baba?'

'Maybe, my little Buzzer,' he says.

'Then I will spray that mosquito with my drone and he'll stop bothering us!'

He smiles: 'But that mosquito you hear will be way up high, like your drone!'

The girl is confused now: 'I don't know, I don't know.'

He gives his daughter a kiss. 'What I do know is: first you must finish your homework. Come on, habeebti, we have to go soon.'

Throwing her bag over her shoulders, the girl heads out onto the street with her father; there they part ways, the girl running and skipping all the way to school – al-Shatea Camp Primary School. She arrives early and kills time in front of the gates by singing to herself, leaning against the school's high wall. She has to wait for the children from the 'morning school' to file out, before she can go in as part of the 'afternoon school'.[2] The morning school is crowded with refugee students. The sound of their voices floods into the street, passing through classroom windows and carrying all the way to the gates and beyond, reminding passers-by that they too once sat in hot, crowded classrooms, playing the same games, screaming the same screams. Then suddenly the playground fills with children: skinny girls in striped uniforms with white ribbons in their braided hair; boys in blue shirts and jeans, kicking footballs or fighting, stuffing their faces with all varieties of snack – sweet, salt and sour – waiting for the gates to open.

Ali is running down the street as fast as he can. He has just finished his shift; these days he works as a florist in Gaza, and has his own shop – 'The Love Ambassador' – on al-Wehda Street. He heads north in the direction of Shifa Hospital, then turns west towards al-Wehda Tower. He needs to get there before Zahra starts class. She's like a daughter to him. He carries a white lily with him as he runs, and is almost there.

Tel Aviv

A thirty-year-old man with delicate features is driving his car down Dizengoff Street. He's listening to the *Voice of Israel* on the radio. Today it's broadcasting the words of Mahmoud Darwish, as interpreted by the famous Lebanese singer Majida El Roumi. It's been nearly two years now since the July War rocked her country.

He recognises snatches of the original poem:
I dreamt of white lilies, an olive branch, a bird embracing the dawn in a lemon tree.
– And what did you see?
– I saw what I did: a blood-red boxthorn.
I blasted them in the sand... in their chests... in their bellies.

The words draw him in, and he turns the radio up.

Homeland for him, he said, is to drink my mother's coffee,
to return safely, at nightfall.

More scattered verses, he drives faster:

I love it with my gun...
...that doves might flock through the Ministry of War...
...that doves might flock...[3]

His car pulls up outside the military base known as Matcal
Tower in the HaKirya quarter. As he reports for duty,
unlikely memories from many years ago intertwine with
his thoughts. *It must be the song*, he thinks.

Throwing open the door to his office, he plonks himself
down in front of the large screen showing a live, black
and white aerial view of a man walking through crowded
streets. He puts a communications headset on and wraps his
right hand around the joystick. He communicates with a
colleague in Hebrew with a strong French accent.

'So? What's up?'

'Your orders are to follow the subject. He's heading
west through al-Shatea Camp. He should be right in front
of you.' And so, another day in the office begins: he watches
his target, like a character in a computer game.

On the screen, the man can be seen approaching al-
Shatea Camp School as he receives a phone call.

'The lilies have blossomed, Ali. It's time.'

The operator with the French accent touches a button
on his headset: 'Possibly a coded message.'

'Neutralise the target. There's no room for error,' comes
the reply.

The operator pauses for a moment, the light from
the screen flickering across his face. The city is like a map

unrolling between his delicate fingers, street after street scrolling towards him. He centres on his target and zooms in, until the colours of the target's clothes, the way he walks, even the flip-flops on his feet can be seen clearly. Then he stops; the man is carrying something in his left hand: it looks like a flower, a lily perhaps. The image of an Arab teenager with a deep dimple in his left cheek glimmers in his mind. 'That was years ago,' he thinks out loud. 'Why am I thinking of that?'

The operator's eyes scan the screen closely, as if hoping to take in every movement, pixel by pixel. From this elevation, the children gathering outside the school gates look like bees swarming around a hive, the man with the flower like some kind of victim being swallowed up by it. The drone's buzzing seems to irritate some of the children: a girl leaning against the school wall covers her ears as she crouches. The man with the flower and the dimple walks towards her. The operator feels his hands growing clammy; his fingers lose their grip on the joystick. He adjusts his grip and tries to focus. The clearer the operator sees his target, the more he hesitates. Children are zigzagging around the target. The operator touches his headset again: 'The target is surrounded by multiple civilians. Please advise?'

'Take down the target. That's an order. Use what caution you can, but follow the order.' The operator's eyes sting with salt.

Zahra spots Ali's face approaching among the children. She turns towards him and peels herself off the school wall. He smiles and waves the white lily, the dimple in his left cheek sinking deeper than ever. For a moment, she forgets the buzzing and the humming and the chaos, and is comforted by the fact that Uncle Ali has come to see her. He calls out to her: 'Zahra, it's your flower! For Mother's Day!'

The man with the French accent lifts his thumb to the button at the top of the joystick, caressing it for a moment. Suddenly the target is clear, the children surrounding the man with the flower have dispersed. He doesn't hesitate; the figure on the screen drops to the pavement.

It all happens in a split second. Zahra is blown backwards by a blast of hot air. Her first thought is that she's been hit by a motorbike. For a moment she can see only smoke. Then, as she gets to her feet, she realises these aren't exhaust fumes. As the smoke clears white petals appear scattered across the pavement. And in between all the white, patches of red. Not flat spots of it, but pieces. Clumps. Threads and stems of red. The humming above her fades. She looks up at the sky. Birds quietly scatter. Something about their silence makes her stiffen like plaster. She can't feel her feet.

The operator takes his thumb off the button. He isn't sweating anymore, and his eyes no longer sting. As he directs the drone north, he gets out his mobile phone with his left hand, and starts to look at possible destinations for his upcoming holiday. Tuscany is meant to be beautiful. He's never been there before.

Notes

1. In 1997, Gaza was occupied by Israeli forces, and there was less of a distinct, hard border between Gaza and the rest of Israel, as both were regarded by the occupiers as one and the same territory; so movement by Gazan Palestinians in and out of Gaza was possible (e.g. commuting to work in Tel Aviv). Following the Israeli disengagement from Gaza, or 'Hitnatkut', in 2005, the hard border between the two territories returned and has remained impenetrable to anyone without a permit to cross through the Erez border. Thus in 2008, commuting from Gaza to Tel Aviv would have been impossible.

2. Due to lack of resources and space, different schools in Gaza often occupy the same building; dividing their use of the building into morning and afternoon slots.

3. Lines from the poem 'A Soldier Dreams of White Lilies' by Mahmoud Darwish (1967), published in English in *Unfortunately, It Was Paradise* (University of California Press, 2003). Translated and edited by Munir Akash and Carolyn Forché.

Our Milk

King David Hotel, Jerusalem
22 July 1946

THEY MARCH IN SINGLE file, dressed in white kitchen uniforms, their sandals dragging under the weight of their churns. A precious cargo: fresh, foamy milk for the hotel's guests. As they set them down, each face seems to betray a different breed of expression to those borne by the frenetic morning cooks. They are surly, somehow, and lacking the air of gentility that hangs over the hotel's own staff. The clatter of spoons and saucers fills the basement kitchen: the ovens are already roaring with heat, the aroma of fresh bread filling the air with the excitement of morning.

Birds swoop past the high windows heading up to where their song will stir the sleepers floors above, rouse them to the smell of incense that lines the hotel's corridors, and the peeling of the Dormicon Church bells half a mile away. The Al Aqsa's call to prayer mingles with the Christian bells and the organ music of the other churches in an existential harmony that soon has everyone out of bed and preparing for the day ahead.

A British soldier leaves his superior's room, muttering to himself as he climbs the hotel's stairs. He is angry, his words barely coherent. 'How could they? Would they really attempt this?'

Seated at a table in the ground-floor restaurant, a woman smiles, lost in thought. With her blonde hair, cherry lipstick and white dress, she looks almost like a movie star, waiting for the glass of fresh milk that has become her morning custom. Her mother-tongue is English, but she knows enough Arabic words to ingratiate herself with the staff.

Surrounded by all the finery of the restaurant, which calls itself 'La Regence', her second morning ritual is to lose herself in the Assyrian tapestry hanging on the wall. In the foreground, in front of the great Phoenician wall that stands as a horizon, she sees all the achievements of the ancients: the wisdom of Greece, the arrogance of Rome, the resplendent beauty of Egypt: a pharaonic barge gliding down a river that meanders between one pink limestone column and another, columns that hold the tapestry taut, as if spooling it impossibly slowly. A cedar tree coils around a lofty column at the edge of the tapestry, lifting the English woman's thoughts with its branches, drawing them upwards, spiralling to a kind of ecstasy that she has discovered too late in life.

The tapestry's vision of the ancient world transports the restaurant's clientele back to a time when theories about how we should live our lives were still contended, still being formulated, when empires could choose what gods to serve, but not be defined by them. When things weren't yet fixed.

'Where's my milk?' the blonde woman asks one of the staff, in Arabic, annoyed by the delay.

'Don't worry, Ma'am. It's on its way – that fresh cream you British love so much.' The waiter's teeth sparkle as he speaks.

The woman smiles back, demonstrating her patience.

As the kitchen clock strikes noon, milk sprays upwards into the air. For a nanosecond of frozen time it mingles with moats of unignited potassium nitrate, sulphur and charcoal. Something that looked like just another churn has exploded, sending the western half of the hotel – its chandeliers, its staircases, its marble floors, its plastered ceilings, and all of its guests – several feet into the air. When this leap is over, the sunlight attempting to break through into its aftermath cannot reach down deep enough to see the smile that still lingers on the English woman's face. Nor to her shoes, buried beneath tons of limestone, now badged with red and white.

The waiter staggers for a moment, still standing in the rear half of the restaurant that hasn't collapsed. His face gushes with blood – some invisible piece of shrapnel has sliced his cheek – but he barely notices it. All he can do is stare at the splashes of colour that fringe the rubble: strips of tapestry and flesh, both heavy with history.

Sbarro's Restaurant, Jerusalem
9 August 2001

Her hair, as black as a misbaha bead, trails in the morning air as she drives down Ramallah-Jerusalem Road with the window down. Her eyes are fixed on the tarmac ahead with a quiet resolve that has stayed with her since she made her decision to give up on journalism in Jordan, and return to the fight. Sitting beside her is a young man, maybe seventeen years old, who says nothing, but gazes at her curiously. Every minute or so, he rubs his hands together; his palms are so coarse she can hear his skin scratching like sandpaper. For a moment, she can't imagine anything dirtier than those hands. Then she notices the clothes he is wearing.

After two further checkpoints, and many more minutes of scratching, they are almost there. As they enter the suburbs, she stops the car and turns to him. One hard stare into his eyes and he seems to relax. The nervous, curious gaze dissipates into a smile, so she reaches behind her seat and brings forward a ukulele case.

'Take this,' she says. 'Carry it over your shoulder when you get out.' She twists her body round again then straightens, this time holding a bumbag. She hands it to him. It looks like a camera bag attached to a belt. 'This is yours also, I believe.' He takes them both and sets them down on his lap, looking ahead with as much focus as she had when she was driving. The car starts up again.

Jaffa Road, dissecting the city from east to west, is its usual cacophony of noise; the clamour of modernity bouncing between ancient city walls: a bustle of street vendors, shoppers, and other obviously low-paid workers, slows the pace of the traffic, their feet crisscrossing in every direction, but all at the same tempo.

The journalist's car nudges its way towards downtown. At the junction of King David Street and Jaffa Road, the young man gets out, throwing the ukulele case over his shoulder and buckling his belt. As he walks towards a cheap-looking café diagonally opposite, the woman realises she'll never know if there's a real ukulele in there, or if he has any musical ability himself. The café is called Sbarro's: it's heaving but he isn't deterred.

A man sitting behind the counter looks up to see the seventeen-year-old eagerly sidestepping those less focussed in their queuing. He tries to smile but an old facial injury makes it look more like a sneer these days. 'Young man, I can see you're hungry,' he calls out cheerfully, 'but relax, we have all the food you can wish for.'

The young man clears his throat as he reaches the counter. 'Yes, I hear you're renowned for your spaghetti,' he replies in Hebrew. 'I'm spoilt for choice. I'm not sure what to have.'

'You've come to the right place. How about pasta with a white garlic sauce? We use a special milk for the sauce,' the old man explains, struggling to wrap his lips around the words. 'Or a spicy red arrabiata?'

'I think I'll have the white sauce,' the young man replies, sitting himself down at a table.

'I was a soldier you know,' the old man says, gesturing at his scar. 'I took part in the single, greatest military act of independence.'

'Yes, I can see that,' the young man grumbles without looking up.

'So, you noticed my injury, eh?' the old man laughs.

'It's too loud in here, I can't hear you,' the young man says, pointing to his ear.

A little boy with freckles, from another table, walks towards him, his eyes set on the ukulele case. Flustered, the young man tries to move it out of his reach without saying anything.

'What's the matter?' the old man calls out, as the waiter brings out his pasta. 'Are small guitars more expensive the normal sized ones?'

'*Kelb*,'[1] the little boy's mother mutters lovingly, as he sits back down beside her. For a moment, the Arabic word confuses the young man. Then a woman in a short skirt walks past his table, carrying a glass of fresh orange juice with plenty of ice. She sits down two tables across from him. Latin music fills the café; the late morning sun dazzles the customers every time they look up.

'Look at those legs!' the old man says.

The young man blushes. The sweat on his skin feels like blocks of ice melting on a griddle pan.

'Seems I'm the younger of the two of us...' the man chuckles.

The teenager stares down at his bowl of pasta and white sauce, as his right hand makes its way to the coarse fabric casing attached to his belt.

As the kitchen clock ticks noon, the white sauce sprays upwards, mingling for a frozen nanosecond with the red. The little boy with freckles daydreams for the last time about learning the guitar. The old man taps his foot to one last beat. The woman with the long legs takes her last sip of orange juice in a tornado of spaghetti and wood and stone. Tables fly, the roof collapses, blood and bone are scattered in the dust. Of the young man's curious gaze, nothing remains. Even the journalist who gave him a lift will fail to remember the look in his eyes, as he rubbed his hands.

Sbarro's Restaurant is demolished but Jaffa Road remains, dissecting the city from east to west with its usual cacophony of noise.

Note

1. *Kelb*: Dog, used affectionately in Arabic, for small children.

14 June[1]

Balcony

SHE FOLLOWS HER LITTLE sister's gaze, as her eyes dart to every new sound in the street below. She can hear her sister's heavy breathing, and wants to hug her, but can't bring herself to do it. Their university is closed today so they have to stay where they are. They stand there together, pressed against the balcony railing, the sound of the TV news filling the apartment behind them.

Through the glare of the sun, she also follows every movement. A woman holding a small, stunted pot plant is running down the road so fast that her slippers keep coming off. It seems she took it from one of the buildings in the square, at the crossroads that leads to the city's administrative headquarters. Her throat is dry as her eyes follows the figure; saliva seems to stick at the back of her throat as she struggles to catch her breath.

Her younger sister points to a group of young men scaling the side of the building opposite and crawling along its roof; they begin to remove the slates, one by one, until the building is left rudely naked to the sky above. She tries to distract her: 'Look at this guy,' and they watch as a man carrying a large aluminium window frame runs down the street, then throws it onto the back of a cart already laden down with plunder. It is like the End Times; people swarm with their loot; official documents change hands, as if to make it official, and every man turns a blind eye to the next; carts and donkeys cluster along the pavements. Others scatter on foot with their acquisitions, emptying buildings that were only abandoned by employees a few hours before.

Allahu Akbar, Allahu Akbar, the looters chant in gratitude, as they bow down at the entrance to the headquarters before entering. God has made them victorious over the infidels.

The sound of the last days' gunfire still rings in the sisters' ears. The family have spent a week in hiding, sleeping in the corridor, staying clear of windows and never daring to go out, for fear their paths might intersect with that of a stray missile or a ricocheted bullet.

Images flash through her mind like lightning. How many times has she jumped out of bed thinking that a bullet has punctured her window? How many times have she and her sister thrown themselves into their mother's arms, or huddled together at the foot of the bed, on hearing an RPG mortar screeching towards that building on the square?

There's a man being held by armed men on the roof of the apartment block across the street; they are dangling him over the edge, his long beard trailing down to the street below.

'What are you doing?' comes a shout from beneath. 'He's one of us!'

The *Voice of Israel* radio can be heard from a nearby balcony: 'Israel has sent ambulances to the nearest border point and is willing to treat Palestinians wounded by the infighting. The gates have been opened to anyone fleeing the violence.' The presenter's words mingle with those shouted by the other men below, as they load their trucks with boxes full of guns. Looking more closely, the older sister can make out faint letters printed onto the side of one of the boxes. She knows the words from her English class.

A fire in one building, smoke snaking upwards from another.

Her legs are a little shaky today, so she paces to and fro along the railing, to walk it off. Her little sister is too nervous to stand at the railing, but she has never been scared of falling, and whenever something new happens, she's quick to lean over the edge as low as she can to make it out.

Groups of masked men are now confiscating their neighbours' cars, declaring them ill-gotten gains, the fruits of corruption, invalid property.

There is a knock at the door. The sisters' mother heads out of the sitting room, where she has been going about her business as if nothing was happening, and answers the door.

'We need to search the house,' a voice says.

'No. It isn't appropriate; my daughters are at home.' She is defiant.

The man at the door starts to raise his voice at her, but another interjects. 'As you wish, Ma'am,' he says. 'We shan't come in. Is there a man in the house?'

'No, nobody's here,' she replies.

'Are there any weapons in the house?'

'No, of course not!'

A bearded man in a khaki jacket suddenly pushes his way through the group. One of the men raises his hand to greet him. 'Get the hell out of here!' he barks. 'Dismissed. This is my brother's house.' The men scatter, like the beads of a dropped misbaha.

Their mother simply walks back to the kitchen. 'Why don't you wait and have lunch with us?' she calls back to him. 'I have to make it early, we're all home anyway.'

Their uncle drops down in front of the television and looks over at his nieces, who have now sat down quietly in front of him. They look older. It seems odd to him that they haven't welcomed him with hugs and blessings, but then he realises he can't bring himself to greet them either. Instead, he just turns up the TV.

One of the reports sends a smile dancing across his face, and it doesn't go unnoticed by the older niece. Getting up, she walks to the coffee table where he has just set down his gun, and hands it back to him. 'Don't leave this lying around the house,' she snaps. 'Keep it holstered. Where is Baba?'

'He's alright. Don't worry. He'll be back,' he replies.

Their uncle puts the gun away.

'Did they take the gun?' he shouts to their mother.

'No, it's safe. It didn't belong to them, and we are staying put anyway. We're not leaving the city just because others are.'

Peephole

She ignites one of the rings on the stove. Instead of setting a pot on it, she stares at it for a moment. If someone else were to enter the kitchen then, they'd think she were counting the number of flames dancing around its circle. One, two, three, four... Her black, almond-shaped eyes are lost in them, as if lost in the distance.

She leaves the gas burning, quickly picks up a knife, and starts chopping vegetables without looking. She tips these into a pot, adds water and lifts the now heavy pot onto the flames. Turning down the gas, she walks out of the kitchen.

She stands behind the balcony door, unseen, observing the way her daughters' bodies react to each new sound. On nearby balconies, neighbours stand perfectly still, like wax statues. Every few seconds there's a crash as something heavy hits the ground below, or lands on a cart. *They should move more*, she thinks. *They should flinch.*

Walking back across the sitting room, she can't help catch more of what the TV has to show of the chaos down below. *Breaking news indeed*, she thinks, ironically. Without making a sound, she reaches the front door and looks through the peephole. Masked men are shouting at a neighbour across the landing, while others carry guns out of her apartment. She sees her neighbour trembling, wringing a teacloth between her hands as she stands there. She can't read her lips so she puts her ear to the door. She catches the odd word... *my husband... travelling to Ramallah.*

She is worried. Her eyes grow wider and her face darkens. Pulling at her hair, she walks to her bedroom, quietly shuts the door behind her, finds her mobile phone and calls her husband. His phone is switched off, but she tries again all the same. Then, remembering the food on the stove, she darts back to the kitchen to find the water boiling over. Snatching the pot away, she scalds herself. Even after running her hand under the cold tap for three minutes, she still wants to scream.

Returning to the peephole, she sees more masked men trudging in and out of her neighbour's apartment, as the woman stands there, motionless. Back in the sitting room, she can hear men ordering the confiscation of cars in the street below. Through the window, she sees two masked men standing guard outside her own apartment block.

After silently checking on the girls, she once more locks herself in her bedroom and digs out her phone. 'Where are you? Your brother is not back yet. Can you hurry back? It's just me and the girls and I see men outside.'

She stops.

'Someone's knocking, I have to go.'

She takes a deep breath, looks at herself in the mirror and pulls her hair back.

We have been through worse, she tells herself. *This will pass and soon it will be as if nothing ever happened today.* She makes secret fists with her hands as she walks to the door. She looks through the peephole. The masked men have arrived.

'We need to search the house.'

'No. It isn't appropriate; my daughters are at home.' She is defiant.

The man at the front starts to raise his voice at her, but another interjects. 'As you wish, Ma'am, he says. 'We shan't come in. Is there a man in the house?'

'No, nobody's here!' she replies.

'Are there any weapons in the house?'

'No, of course not.'

A bearded man in a khaki jacket suddenly pushes his way through the group. One of the men raises his hand to greet him. 'Get the hell out of here!' he barks. 'Dismissed. This is my brother's house.' The men scatter, like the beads of a dropped Misbaha.

She simply walks back to the kitchen. 'Why don't you wait and have lunch with us?' she calls back to him. 'I have to make it early, we're all home anyway.'

He follows her in and shuts the door. 'Don't worry, he's alright,' he whispers.

She stops and turns around to face him.

'Yes, I think so. The girls are inside. Go check on them, will you.'

She walks into the kitchen and starts to cry. Her first time today. Then, just as quickly, she wipes her face, lights the stove and starts to cook, this time not looking at the flames.

Note

1.   The title refers to 14 June 2007, the day in which Palestinian president Mahmoud Abbas announced the dissolution of the unity government and declared a state of emergency. It occured at the height of the Battle of Gaza, also referred to as 'Hamas' takeover of Gaza' (10–15 June 2007), which followed Fatah losing the parliamentary elections of 2006. Hamas fighters took control of the Gaza Strip and removed Fatah officials from political and aministrative positions, resulting in the de facto division of the Palestinian territories into two entities, the West Bank governed by the Palestinian National Authority, and Gaza governed by Hamas.

The Long Braid

IF SHE LEANS BACK far enough in her chair, behind her modest desk on the fourth floor, she can just about see the sky. The windows of the office are always open, and when she pushes back away from the desk, her cheeks are touched by a cool breeze as soft as the white curtains billowing above her. She smiles as she listens to the music in the background. She takes a sip of her coffee and starts to write today's article. It is Land Day[1] and the office smells of spring. On the desk in front of her sits a computer and monitor, but the keyboard is pushed to one side, to make space for her notebook. She always starts with her notebook. Whatever she's writing about – whether it's the latest announcement from Ramallah, or a new report on the state of the Strip's water supply – she always starts her day with an exercise: a visualisation of some ancient memory, just to get her mind into the quiet space needed to write. She closes her eyes.

The sound of applause washes over her. She tightens her grip on the microphone, feels her hands slowly warming its cold metal.

She opens her eyes and looks down at the pen currently gripped in her fingers. For a moment she continues to hold it like a microphone, then remembers where she is and begins to scribble down the opening paragraph of her article. Before long she has three pages of notes. Taking another sip of coffee, she sets the notebook down and pulls the keyboard towards her.

Her delicate fingers flit across the keyboard, as if performing a piece of music at a piano. From time to time, she pauses, to toy with her newly cut hair, passing its thick strands between her fingers. Whenever she types, her body moves rhythmically in her chair, as if remembering some melody. Her feet rest on the floor beneath her on tiptoes, as if poised to begin a new routine. Her whole body is limber.

Suddenly, the memory of her French dance instructor swims into her thoughts. The woman had given her tap dance lessons: 'No, I'm an Arab.' She smiles at the memory.

She sits back in her chair and wonders about other talents she might have developed. As a girl, she'd also had a singing coach, an American. She touches her throat gently for a moment, unsure if she can still sing the way she once did. Instead, she tries to look at what she's writing now through his eyes, the singing coach's. *Would he have seen music in it?*

Twenty years have passed since she last sung in front of other people, but every time she imagines it, her pulse races and she feels a lump in her throat that she cannot swallow. This triggers, in turn, something else, and she feels tears stinging her eyes, like the ones she tried so desperately not to shed that day she was excluded from class. With each new sting, she writes down another word on a blank page of the notebook; a word that describes her love for her country, a word that stands in defiance of all the meaningless symbols her maths teacher put on the board that day.

30 March 1997

A long braid swings behind Qamar, like a tail. Her feet hardly seem to touch the floor as she skips down the corridor of the UNRWA[2] school in the standard black and yellow stripes of the refugee children's uniforms. But for the fact that she is late for class, she has all the grace of a butterfly.

She knocks on the classroom door nervously. 'Can I come in?' she asks.

'Where have you been?' the maths teacher snaps as she teases the door open. He is a short, fat man with thick-framed glasses and on this particular day a very colourful shirt.

'I was rehearsing for the school show,' Qamar explains.

Mr Ibrahim fires her a quizzical look, amused by the girl's rebelliousness.

'You know, on judgement day, you'll hang from that braid of yours? Not to mention smoulder in the fires of hell for leaving it exposed? Your voice should be put to better use, like reciting the holy Qur'an.'

Her cheeks flush but her eyes hold his gaze. She doesn't hate this teacher; in fact, she rather likes him. 'But it's Land Day, sir,' she explains, still standing in the doorway. 'And I want to participate in the singing of patriotic songs.'

The exchange grows more animated, and the other girls watch in awe as Qamar rebuffs and returns each of her teacher's accusations. Finally he relents and allows her to enter the classroom. She walks to her chair confidently, as all the other girls smile at her, without quite knowing why. She smiles back at them all, and sits down.

A few hours later and the Land Day celebrations are well under way. Qamar doesn't hesitate to volunteer to speak at a large gathering of teachers and students outside the school gates. In her opening words, she improvises freely but from time to time slows down and returns to specific lines of poetry she had rehearsed for this occasion. Her science teacher, Mr Rafiq, whispers words of encouragement from behind her. 'Hold the microphone closer, grip it properly,' he instructs. 'Keep going, Qamar; don't stop.' She nods and smiles back at the crowd, continuing. Some of the other teachers on the podium start to grow impatient.

The time comes for her to finish with a rendition of a patriotic song. It is one her uncle taught her when she first arrived in Gaza, as one of the 'Returned'.[3] He had sung it to her under the lemon and olive trees that her grandfather planted in the camp garden.

When she finishes, a roar of applause crashes over her. Mr Rafiq steps up and hugs her: 'I'm so proud of you, daughter Qamar.' He is a tall and wiry man, with a thick moustache. But he is also kind.

As soon as she gets off the podium, the maths teacher marches up to her. 'We need to have a talk, Qamar,' he says sarcastically, with a hint of admiration. She nods to show that she understands and follows him to his office. Once inside, she waits for him to sit down behind his desk, but he doesn't; he just stands in front of her and looks her up and down. 'Qamar, when are you going to stop with this nonsense?' He spits his words and she can feel the moisture of his rage as it hits her face. He rants, and rants and rants, but soon she can no longer hear the words, just watches his lips and teeth move silently up and down, up and down, until she cannot see him at all. When it's over, she leaves and goes home to cry in her room.

This was before her parents forbad her from dancing, of course. She had been taking dancing and singing lessons led by a delegation of international volunteers, called 'Heart to Heart'. The group had come to Gaza to teach refugee children about performance and creativity.

'There's no tolerance in the community for what you're doing, Qamar,' her mother shouts at her later that evening. 'It isn't accepted here. Your father can't handle the criticism from the people he works with, or from his cousins.'

As her mother berates her, she drifts back to that day on the beach, when the smile on her father's face as he watched her dance with the rest of the group couldn't be mistaken. They had been practicing for a show that would take them around the world. The more her father smiled, the easier it was to dance like a butterfly. They thought about all the countries their performance would take them to. That smile of her father's would never leave her just as her country never would.

She loved these after-school groups. In music, she would watch in awe as the American teacher, Jonathan, would take turns playing the guitar one minute, the piano the next. Whenever she finished a rendition, he would tuck a strand of blond hair neatly behind his ear and remove his glasses – a sure sign that he was about to tell her off: 'Open your mouth wider, Qamar. All the way. Don't be embarrassed by the way it looks. The most important thing is for your voice to be heard. You want to sing about this country when you're older, don't you?' She would listen to the sound of her voice as she sang – the high notes and the low ones, she would lose herself in them until there was nothing left of herself but the song.

In dance class it was the same. Qamar loved to watch her instructor's, Lily's, graceful movements. She was always effortlessly elegant and, although a little old, amazingly supple. Lily's hair style seemed a little quirky, and red like her own hair. But her eyes were as soft and soulful as a song.

Lily would place her hand on Qamar's back, and whisper: 'Relax your back but keep it taut. Feel the weightlessness of your body. Bend gently forwards and picture yourself dipping your hands into a river. Feel the droplets of water glisten on your fingers in the sunlight. Feel your hands glide through the water, focus only on those droplets of water. Don't say anything, just dance on the tip of your toes until you lose yourself.'

Then when the exercise was over, she would tell her: 'Now sit, close your eyes, and tell us a story from the dance.'

She wouldn't hesitate to do anything she was asked. That feeling of weightlessness would stay with her for years to come, the image of sunlight twinkling through the drops of water on her fingers. It took her to another place, a place where she was happy. She knew herself better there.

'There's something different about you, Qamar,' the French woman said to her one day. 'Are you from Gaza?'

'I have just moved here from Syria.'

'So you are French!' she exclaims. 'You must speak French?'

Qamar was puzzled by this for a moment. 'No, I'm an

Arab. I'm Palestinian. I know a few French words, but my English is better.'

Unprompted, Lily started to untie Qamar's long braid and comb the hair out straight. Then she picked her up and spun her round. 'You should loosen your hair, let it be free like you. You remind me of my daughter, Qamar... Don't ever stop smiling, you hear me?'

'Qamar, Qamar, Qamar!' The maths teacher is shouting her name.

'I'm here, sir,' she says, back in his office, feeling his spit land on her face as he shouts.

'You're wasting your time with this nonsense! You're better than this. There's no such thing as a patriotic song, you know! All songs are degenerate; your only loyalty is to God, to your religion.'

She fixes him with a long, hard look, seeing only dead eyes and an empty stare, set into a tried, sallow face.

This episode might bring tears to her eyes, later that night in her room, but she knows she has faced worse than this. Like the time he kicked her out of class for standing up to him when he said women who called themselves 'emancipated' were 'sluts'. She is proud of the restraint she showed that day, despite her anger, despite his humiliation of her, in front of the other girls. She can feel the same tears prickling her eyes as she felt then, tears she refused to shed for his ignorance. She left the classroom that day without giving him another look. 'The God I know pays no resemblance to the monster you rant about,' she says with a smile, and proceeded to skip all the way down the corridor and out into the courtyard of the Zeitun Preparatory School for Girls.

Notes

1. Land Day (30 March) – Commemorating the day in 1976 when, in response to the Israeli government's announcement of a plan to expropriate thousands of dunams of land for state purposes, a general strike and marches were organized in Arab towns from the Galilee to the Negev. In the ensuing confrontations with the Israeli army and police, six unarmed Arab citizens were killed, and about one hundred were wounded.

2. The *United Nations Relief and Works Agency*.

3. As part of the Oslo Accord, many thousands of Palestinian refugees and their families, living in refugee camps in Syria and Lebanon, were returned to Gaza in the late 1990s.

The Anklet of Maioumas

IN A LONG, LOOSE-FITTING dress, a figure can be seen dancing between the gigantic columns of the temple. The dappled translucence of her dress blends with the marbled surface of each pillar. The dress trails behind her as she moves – a thin, diaphanous layer of fabric that traces the outline of her frame whenever it settles back around her. Both the swirl of the marble and the whorl of her dance seem to point, spiralling upwards, towards the capitals of each column, and beyond to the domed roof and the oculus at its centre. Leaves from an old olive tree can be seen matted into the girl's hair, which fans out around her shoulders and all the way down to her lower back.

As the figure dances, a faint, tinkling sound can be heard: an anklet, decorated with coins that dangle over the girl's left foot. Nearby, out in the square, or somewhere beyond, a grain mill can also be heard turning and turning its wheel, as if in time to music that only the girl can hear. It picks up speed as her dancing does, spinning between the columns. The coins ring louder, glinting in the temple's shadows, throwing their golden lustre upwards onto her legs.

A third sound accompanies the tinkling of the anklet and the low hum of the basalt stone grinding the wheat: the sound of the sea. A woman with eastern features sits out in the square watching the figure in the temple whirling from column to column, as if this vision represented her destiny, not a past she'd long escaped.

The girl revolves around one column, her right hand pointing to the ceiling above her, her left reaching down, tracing the circumference of the column's lowest stone. To the old woman outside, it seems for a moment as if the whole column is balanced in the palm of the girl's hands, as she spins around it. Seeing the woman looking at her, she calls out: 'Make the mill go faster! I want to see who can spin the fastest!'

The old woman, cloaked in a black dress with the emblem of a bird tattooed on her forehead, laughs. 'It's going as fast as it can. You're too fast for it, Princess.' The girl spins on.

Again the sound of the sea echoes through the square, as if it's coming from the very sky above them. As the mill wheel turns, the anklet chimes deeper and deeper, like the bell above the Maioumas town forum, announcing some imminent danger. Or the bell of a boat caught in a storm, or some vessel already drowned.

At the foot of a mountain crawling with olive trees, a young man looks up across to the sprawling city of Jerusalem. Dressed in ragged, dusty clothes, he tries to make out the Dome of the Rock in the haze, while peeling an apple with a pocket knife. 'Back to work. Let's finish this thing!' his friend shouts. 'Break time is over.' Forgetting his knife, the young man jumps off the rock he's been sitting on, and sets about loading up the heavy stones needed for the foundation of a new settlement.

Back in the coastal city of Maioumas – a city which, thousands of years later, would be discovered by archaeologists wearing diving suits and oxygen masks – the girl's dancing intensifies. In the square outside, a man arrives with a bag of tools, followed by a large block of stone, drawn by a horse and cart flanked by two labourers. As the stone is set in place, he lifts a hammer and chisel, and makes the first blow. 'This will be the entrance to the fortress,' he explains to the woman in black, looking on. 'I carved those columns over there, you know,' he adds, pointing to the temple.

The princess's anklet stops tinkling. At the sound of the chisel's tapping, she rushes to the temple's entrance and stares at the sculptor working on the stone opposite her. The princess freezes, as if she too were one of the columns being shaped by his careful fingers. The mill wheel carries on turning. The old woman watches on with a surreptitious smile. In the silence, she feels her own sweat gathering on her skin. The sculptor is too focussed on his work to notice the noise he is making.

'Slow it down!' the princess yells to the old woman, meaning the mill. This breaks the sculptor's concentration who turns to greet the princess. The princess approaches him, 'Your handiwork is truly marvellous,' she exclaims.

He smiles at this: 'Not as marvellous as the sculptor that made you, Princess.' The sun beams down on her, and the sea calls her name. She runs towards it, abandoning the sculptor.

The young man returns to his rock after a hard day's lifting. He has the kind of muscular frame you'd expect of a builder, but his facial features are far more delicate than his co-workers'. Usually in the exhaustion that immediately follows a long day's work, his thoughts start to wander to a fixed time and place in his memories: the image of a girl running on the beach; she was like an old Roman princess untouched by history, but given to the sea of Gaza like a precious offering. He can almost see the girl dancing before his eyes, and smell her feet on the ancient sands. He bends to pick up some soil then rubs it between his hands.

The horse's neigh reaches her, and she has a sudden yearning for the smell of damp, fresh hay. The princess goes to feed her horse but, as she approaches, hears the faint sound of sighs and whispers coming from a nearby stable. Slowly she steps towards it, careful not to make a sound. She glimpses through a narrow crack in the wall, and there, lying among the hay, is her sculptor. His nimble fingers move, not on a marble column, but on the ivory legs of a woman, glinting in the rays of sunlight that steal in through the cracks. His fingers move slowly and slyly like a mill wheel turning and grinding on nothing. She listens to the woman's groans and sighs, and the sculptor's whispers. It is the stable master's daughter. The horse neighs nearby as if sobbing over a broken heart.

A girl sits on an outcrop of ruined wall, half-submerged in the sands of Gaza's beach. In a pool of tide water, trapped in one of its crevices, she has spent many hours inspecting her reflection, half pretending it was the face of an ancient princess, looking up at her through the ages. Between the rock pool and the waves out on the horizon, she has imagined the princess to be very much like her. Today, though, her eyes are itching and she finds it hard to focus: the image in the water keeps breaking up, as if the rocks themselves were shaking. The girl rouses herself suddenly, as if waking up from a nightmare.

For the first time, she feels the sun in her eyes, and notices the edges of the wall she has been sitting on are sharp and uncomfortable. She hadn't felt any discomfort till now. She looks at the sky and thinks how beautiful and distant it is, and gets to her feet, feeling back to her normal self again – not cramped and shrunken and hemmed in, the way she does in the narrow confines of the city. Here she is free, full size. Free to wear trousers, not a dress. Free to run in the wind, with only the sound of the ancient mill ringing in her ears. Then a café up on the promenade distracts her, with its noisy TV spewing out the day's news, and everything comes back to her: It was an ancient mill they discovered, out on the seabed. They reported it on Al Quds TV.

The young man returns to his perch on the slopes of Abu-Ghoneim Mountain, and gazes down, beyond a high wire-fence, at a group of Israeli men chatting to their girlfriends in the park below. This rock feels like a cage to him, and these men are like wild birds free to fly outside it, wherever they choose.

He remembers his girlfriend's tearful words to him: 'When am I going to break through that border? When will they give me a permit to come and see you?' Other voices crowd his mind, like the sound of his father's voice: 'You don't have to wait for her to come. You only spent a few days in Gaza; how can you say you're committed to her? The situation has changed, son, they have stopped letting ordinary civilians pass through Erez. Our lives and our work are here: I build the wall and you build settlements. Wake up from your daydreams, boy!' There were the other sounds crowding his thoughts as well, sounds he wished he didn't hear: drums and whistles, the clamour of festivities surrounding his eventual wedding to his cousin.

The girl runs across the beach, crying. She has missed out on life, she realises. Too many years have been lost in isolation, disconnected from the world. Years wasted waiting for permission to be reunited with her lover.

She had waited for him and felt sure that, one day, despite everything, they would be together again. But when the princess had seen her beloved sculptor in the stables in Maioumas, lying with another woman, the girl who had created her knew that the waiting must come to an end. Why wasn't it clear to her on the land, what had become obvious out there, in the depths of the sea?

The bars of this cage can be broken, the man decides, bending down once more to touch the soil in the shadow of his rock. Only this time, his fingers aren't satisfied with just a handful of dirt, they scratch deeper and deeper, until they strike something hard and cold. A metal box. As he retrieves it from the soil and opens it, his throat tightens. The text imprinted along the barrel seems oddly familiar: *92 FS BERETTA*. He passes it from one hand to the other for a moment, getting used to its weight. Then he takes aim. He chooses a young Israeli teenager skipping around his girlfriend in the park below, like two birds blissfully ignorant of the fact that they're being hunted. A gunshot echoes across the valley. Then another.

The coins on the girl's anklet begin to jangle loudly as she runs across the beach. The sound of the mill wheel's relentless grinding grows louder. *Grains are being scattered everywhere*, she thinks. Then there is a great noise, like a crack of thunder, as the wheel comes off its axis and hits the lower floor, then another as it falls flat on its side. What a cacophony. *Or is it the sound of gunfire*, she thinks. The anklet continues to jangle and tinkle and ring above the wet sands of Gaza beach, but against the crashing of the waves in the distance, no one can hear it but her.

Breastfeeding

Farewell Party, June 2008

YARA'S GRANDMOTHER HITS THE ground with her cane. Dressed in a humble, peasant thobe with traditional embroidery and a white scarf covering her thick, grey hair, she looks like a messenger from an ancient world. Her fierce eyes are devoid of the tenderness you'd expect from someone looking at their granddaughter, especially one dancing so gracefully as she is now. Yara's thin frame sways like a young, green branch, her blonde hair fanning down her back like a palm leaf. The girl is paying no attention to her surroundings, or the moment she finds herself in. Instead, she is imagining the streets and the people of Paris, and what the long journey to that distant city might entail. The grandmother, with her miserly, wrinkled face smacks the ground with her cane once more. Yara's mother turns to look at her mother-in-law's cane for a moment, then she looks back at her daughter, radiant as the sun at noon. Her little one has grown up so fast and here she is: a bride dancing before her, a bride dreaming of Paris.

Bedtime, May 1978

Thirteen-year-old Sara sits in the corner of their family's one-room shack, the walls of which are made of mud, roofed by sheets of corrugated iron. Beneath her, spread across the floor, is a cold, plastic mat; she supports herself with a pillowcase stuffed with old clothes, her head deep in her school notebooks, revising. All her spare time is spent this way: her eyes down – studying, or up – dreaming. Of travel, of going to university in Cairo, of escaping Jabalia. The camp's sandy alleyways have so far only led her round in circles, like a maze, always back to where she started. The only route that didn't feel like it was a trick was the one to school each morning. She strode towards it, proudly, rebelliously, convinced it would lead her out of there, in the end, to finish her studies elsewhere.

She cannot hear the chaos of her five sisters running around her, in a room that doubles as a bedroom, study, and kitchen. She is too engrossed in her books. Nor can she hear her mother's continual nags and calls for assistance. Until, one day, the unexpected happens. Her aunty, the one with the frightening eyes and gravelling voice, has come to the house asking for the strangest thing: the girl's hand in marriage for her son. 'We have decided that your daughter, Sara, would make an adequate wife for our third son, Fouad, and we expect you, as a family, to accept this offer.'

Her parents look embarrassed, then their expressions turn to something else. They fear for her, Sara realises. They fear she will become entangled in the traditions that they themselves were raised with and could never escape. 'You have to marry your cousin, Fouad,' they announce after her aunty has left. Years from now, all she will remember of that day is her screaming; a dizzying memory of wailing, pulling at her hair, pounding her fists against the mat. 'He hasn't even finished school! What about my studies? What about Cairo?'

June 2008

She smacks the floor again with her cane, scaring the guests assembled near her. Then she rises from her plastic chair and, in a voice that cuts through the clamour of the guests singing and clapping to the old village songs, she hisses at her bride's mother: 'What were you thinking, Sara? Where has your undisciplined brain wandered to? Sending your daughter to Paris to marry a husband 20 years older than her! She's only nineteen, for goodness sake...'

Sara stirs from her thoughts. 'You don't have a say in anything to do with my daughter,' she shouts back. 'Have you forgotten? I was her age. Younger in fact!'

Yara makes her way gently through the crowd and embraces her mother. 'Listen,' she says, turning to her grandmother, 'Mama had nothing to do with my decision. I wouldn't marry a cousin, even if he was my age. That's all you care about, keeping the family together, not how old I am or my husband is. This is *my* life.'

Border Crossing, February 2009

Yara has been waiting for hours. Her name is finally on the list of those allowed to leave, but there will be no leaving today. The Rafah crossing is closed already. The cars queuing along the dirt track from early morning have barely moved all day. Their passengers' dreams of escape into Egypt have evaporated, for the day at least, along with the steam rising from their car bonnets. The two Hamas soldiers, sitting in front of the entrance building with their legs crossed, seem to know something all the wannabe travellers don't. Tomorrow, perhaps, not all the places will be taken up by party members, or people with friends in high places.

Yara gives up, and tells the taxi driver to turn around. That college professor in Paris will have to wait for her yet another day. He decided to marry Yara without even coming to Gaza; his parents arranged the contract, with the help of an Imam in France and one in Gaza, but they have only ever met over MSN Messenger. The traditions of the camp still run in his veins, he says, even though he hasn't set foot in Palestine in decades. But with each new delay, the rumours of their imminent divorce persist. It has been four months now. Too long to be married and still strangers. The taxi lurches violently, as it drops off the broken tarmac and circles round in the dust, before remounting the road and heading the other way. *When Rafah opens*, Yara thinks, *it will be heaven's mercy: the earth is too much for me.*

A Telephone Call, January 2009

'What are you doing, habeebti?'

'I'm baking bread.'

Her mother laughs. 'Have you tried French bread yet? They say it's delicious. Don't tell me you're still using that copper skillet like a Gazan peasant, Yara…?'

'I've already told you, Mama. He bought it years ago before going to Paris, he's fond of it,' Yara says, but there is something in her voice that unsettles her mother. Yara falls silent.

'What's wrong?' her mother asks.

Yara lets out a solitary sob, like someone clearing her throat. 'Mama, I never leave the house. I don't know what Paris is like.'

'Oh, habeebti, what have I done to you? I should have never agreed to this marriage...'

'Don't say that, Mama,' Yara comforts her. 'I was the one who wanted to marry him. We all have to grasp at the chances we can in this life.'

A Knock at the Door, February 2010

Sara takes her foot off the sewing machine peddle and waits for the noise to die down. When she eventually gets up to open it, there is a woman standing in the corridor with a baby in her arms. 'Yara!' she cries, after a moment of stunned silence. She hugs them both and doesn't completely let go until all three of them are over the threshold and well into the flat. 'You didn't tell me you were coming back? How long are you staying for? Where's the professor? Is he staying at his cousin's? You should have said, I have no food in...'

'No, Mama, no, wait, look...' Yara hands the girl still sleeping in her arms over to her mother, and takes a long, deep breath. 'I'm divorced, Mama. We've come back to stay.'

For another speechless moment, Sara looks into her daughter's dark green eyes. 'Thank God,' she says eventually. 'You've come back to take care of your mother, now all your ungrateful brothers have abandoned her... I don't even know where they are right now.' The baby in the woman's arms starts to cry, and Sara has to fight back her own tears. 'Of course, and I can teach you both to speak French now too!' Yara smiles.

Breastfeeding, June 2010

'Habeebti, I'm so glad you stuck with the breastfeeding, so many women give up these days.'

'I'm glad too,' Yara smiles. They are sitting on the veranda of their fourth floor apartment, overlooking the Shatilla camp and the sea beyond it. The sun is setting and the cold has started to set in. Yara's mother seems distracted again. She is staring at her daughter's small left breast, and the baby idly latching onto the nipple and gnashing at it for a moment, before spitting it out again.

Sara's thoughts retreat into memories of breastfeeding her own daughter, over 30 years earlier. How the milk would spill out of Yara's mouth whenever she unlatched, and trickle down her delicate neck in tiny white streams. How she would mop up the droplets with her fingertips and lick them. She wanted to taste whatever it was that gave her little girl such comfort. To be comforted with her. She used to tell the girl, 'Pretty Yara, it is a blessing that you didn't inherit your mother's black hair. Your father's fairness will bring you good luck. My black locks never brought me any – except for the day I had you, of course.'

She still remembers the ecstasy of kissing those soft, plump cheeks, and soon finds herself back in the summer of 1986 one afternoon, as the whole family sat around, fanning each other with old newspapers: Yara at her breast and, across from them, the girl's father, Fouad, with his legs stretched out in front, and his head resting on his aunt's – Sara's mother's – lap. Her memory of the scene retains every detail: the old woman knitting a woollen dress for her granddaughter, her ancient needles clicking, every so often pausing to play with her son-in-law's hair. 'Aunty,' Fouad teases her, 'now that I have two sons and a daughter, and

Sara's busy raising them, I want to marry again.'

The needles fly up into the air above him. 'Get off my lap, have you come from behind the cows!'

'But Aunty,' Fouad laughs, 'Sharia permits it. It's halal.'

'What, are you a fan of that polygamous sheikh at the Zarqa Mosque now?'

'What's got into you?' Fouad asks.

'You have Sara and you barely deserve her!' She yells.

'Why don't I?'

Sara looks up at him without saying a word. She doesn't know if he was being serious or not, but she is glad her mother is standing up for her.

'Listen, Fouad,' the old woman continues, retrieving a needle from the floor only to wave at him. 'I agreed to let Sara marry you and not go to university, even though she was the brightest student in the school –'

'I see,' he interrupts her. 'Another chance to rub it in my face that she's better educated than me!'

'No, but you know that's also true. If I wanted to rub your face in it, I wouldn't have accepted you as my son-in-law.'

'It's decided then: I'm going to get myself another wife,' he announces, crossing his arms. 'I'm serious.'

Sara flinches, her nipple slipping from the baby's mouth. Her mother becomes enraged: 'I curse the breast that nursed you till you were full!'

Sara turns pale. 'Mama, what are you saying?' The baby starts to cry.

'*You* breastfed me! That makes me your own son,' Fouad roars in disgust, 'and the brother of my own wife! Do you not know the basics of Sharia?'

A Fatwa, August 1988

For a year or so, Fouad has tried to bury all memory of this conversation under the chatter of daily life. But it's no good. Somehow the old woman's words – *I curse the breast* – bubble up through his thoughts. He starts paying regular visits to his two local mosques, winning the respect of the sheikhs at each. After six months of quiet nodding, reverential agreement, and solemn hand-shaking, he feels confident enough to ask the head sheikh at each mosque a question. 'It is an issue of scripture,' he assures them. 'A clarification.'

'Three separate breastfeeding sessions is sufficient,' the sheikh at the Zarqa Mosque tells him. 'That would make you effectively the "son" of your aunt... and the "sister" of your wife'.

'Technically, five full feeds are required', the sheikh at the 'Ahmar Mosque tells him.

When Sara relays this news back to her mother, the old woman laughs: 'We didn't have the wisdom of Sharia to help us back then! We were still living in a mud-hut, eight people to a room, on the same tiny plot of land that our family's tent had stood on since 1948! My sister was ill; she had no energy to feed the boy. So I had to. For a month. Maybe six weeks. Sharia didn't help us then!'

When Sara lets this slip to her husband one night, he knows he has enough.

'I want more than a clarification, I want a ruling,' he demands of the Zarqa sheikh the following morning, choosing this sheikh because he had one more wife than the other.

And a week later the ruling is issued: an official fatwa to annul their marriage. Fouad waits for the letter to arrive confirming it. When it does, he reads it slowly over breakfast and, once read, jams it into his already-stuffed suitcase. Then he leaves, closing the door on their new, third-floor apartment, with its balcony overlooking the sea; closing the door on ten years of marriage, three children, and his first wife, to go look for a second. But as the door hits its frame, the sound of it wakes Sara, not just from her slumber or her train of thought, but from her whole life. With that sound, she knows what she will do: she will not despair or indeed look for a new husband, she will just sew. Stitch and sew and tear and cut. The sewing machine's whirr will ring in the ears of all her children through all the years ahead, it will drown out the sound of her own regrets and it will keep the house together. As long as its whirring deafens them, they will not hear the bitterness of the mother that brought them into this world.

June 2010

Sara rouses herself. The sun has now set over the Mediterranean, and the restaurant down on the beach has lit its candles. Some are already floating out to sea, mounted in cut-in-half plastic bottles. She looks down at her granddaughter, finally asleep, and up at the baby's mother. 'I will sew, Yara,' she says. 'I will keep sewing. You will finish your studies and we will raise the child together. I will sew until you have a scholarship. I will sew until you escape this wretched camp. I will sew until you are free... in Egypt.'

A Samarland Moon

THEY SIT QUIETLY IN the moonlight on the edge of the promenade wall, the waves of the Mediterranean crashing beneath them. A cold breeze stings their faces, but they keep their distance from each other; a clear gap can be seen between them at all times, like an invisible wall. They both tremble from the cold; the girl's hair billowing upwards, sideways, then in all directions: even towards him at one point. When strands of it brush his face, he thinks he can bear it no longer. Eventually he breaks the silence.

'To me, Rima, you are like the first day of spring.'

For a moment, dimples dent her expression as a smile flickers across her face. She is such a slight girl, a strong gust of wind could take her away. The boy's eyes, meanwhile, are a dark, glassy brown, framed by heavy eyelids and thick lashes.

Ziad is in his first year at university, while Rima is still in high school, a year from graduating. This night, sitting with their feet dangling over the sea wall, will be the beginning of their life together. The beach stretches out in front of them, empty and all theirs: a future to walk across, to feel their sneakers sink into, to watch the moonlight in its troubled distance.

That moonlit night was three years ago. The sky she opens her eyes into now is brighter, and the air she feels against her face, as she peers through the passenger window of Ziad's car, is warmer.

They remain parked for a moment. Having buckled herself in, Rima's delicate hands reach up for the rear-view mirror, and tilt it so she can inspect Ziad's face from a different angle.

'Ziad, look!' she teases. 'In the mirror, all you are is a beard.'

He looks at Rima through the re-adjusted mirror, says nothing for a moment, then nods downwards at her legs: 'I see that as you get older, your trousers get tighter.'

'I told you to stop commenting on my clothes, Ziad. Girls of our generation dress likes this now! Deal with it.'

'So what if all the other girls dress like that? Don't you have a mind of your own to decide what you want to wear?'

'Shall we just go?' Rima sighs. They haven't spent much time together recently and she doesn't want to waste it on an argument.

Ziad starts the car with a tense expression on his face, and pulls out onto the Beach Road. They stop at a red light on the busy Al Remal Street. 'This road could do with being wider,' Rima thinks out loud.

'Like the Strip!' Ziad laughs. A little girl around nine years old, in a school uniform, but with torn slippers on her feet, approaches the car. She knocks on Rima's window, a parcel of faded mint leaves in her hands.

'Please buy my leaves, my little brother is sick and we don't have food at home.'

Rima is incensed. 'Why aren't you in school? Who sent you to sell this?' The girl doesn't respond, but Rima's barrage of questions won't stop.

'Aren't your parents worried about you? Doesn't the school ask where you are? Don't you realise the street is dangerous?'

The girl remains quiet until Rima grabs the mint, gives her some money and orders her to get back to school. Rima can't sit still. She reaches into her bag for a notebook and uses it to fan herself with an impatience that unsettles Ziad.

'Things like this make my blood boil! Tell me, Ziad, what would be better for this poor girl? You being close to God or you straying from the path?'

'How has she got anything to do with me?'

'How has she got anything to do with you...?' she laughs. 'Well nothing, evidently.'

They pass a group of women gathered outside the Red Cross office.

'Ziad, stop the car,' Rima says.

'I think it's a meeting for the families of political prisoners,' he explains, braking. 'I don't know what good these women will do for the cause. Look at them, standing there half naked, shouting. Shame on them.'

'Is that really how you see them? Then I'll get out now and join them, in that case; I'll add my shouting half-nakedness to their cause.'

'Don't! Please, Rima.'

'I'm messing with you. I wouldn't just intrude on their plight like that. But I did want to see their faces,' she says while looking directly at them. 'I can't imagine what it must be like to be a mother separated from her son.'

Ziad stares at Rima for a moment, but doesn't say anything.

She turns the radio on and the sweet sound of Fairuz's voice fills the car. It is a Gaza tradition: Fairuz in the morning, Umm Kulthum in the evening.

Rima sighs, waiting for the verse to end. 'I know you don't like her anymore.'

'Yes, and what's wrong with that? A verse from the Qur'an is more beautiful than any music.'

'That may be true, but there is nothing wrong with music — it's the sounds and rhythms of nature.' She tries to reason but gives up. 'OK, let's go.' Ziad pulls the car carefully out onto Al Rimal Street but within a few blocks he sees a friend from work. The man comes to Ziad's window and jokes with him for a few minutes. When he leaves he casts a silent look of disgust in Rima's direction.

'I saw that, asshole,' Rima mutters under her breath. Ziad has clearly seen it too. 'Screw your friend, he's backwards!'

'Rima, I don't comment on your friends so grant me the same courtesy.'

Rima stays quite for the next few blocks until she sees a man on the other side of the road dressed in court attire. 'I have a lot of respect for that kind of uniform,' she says. 'Black is especially fetching in that cloak.' Then she catches Ziad off guard: 'Why did you study law?'

He carries on driving.

'Ziad, I'm waiting for your answer.'

Sighing and without taking his eyes off the road, he says: 'I don't know, it was the wrong choice, I should have studied Sharia. I have no respect for man's law.'

'Knowledge is accumulative and the law takes from everything. Don't you have any respect for the mind God gave you? You are so strange.'

'What's it to you?' he snaps. 'You just focus on your journalism exams... Stick to writing degenerate articles about me and my friends in your student newspaper.'

'You can't see beyond the end of your nose, Ziad.'

'Just stay out of my business will you!'

'I'm thirsty,' she says, changing the subject. 'Talking to you has that effect. Can you pull over and buy me a bottle of water?'

As he gets out of the car, she mumbles to herself: 'The more backward he gets the fonder I am of him.'

'Here,' he says handing her a bottle when he returns. 'Drink it and try not to talk so much if you have a dry throat.'

'They both smile and Rima seizes her opportunity: 'Hey why don't we go to the photography studio? I want to have a picture taken with you: one of those vintage, black and white ones.' Ziad obediently takes a left and heads towards the city centre. Fifteen minutes later they are in the photography studio on Salah A-Deen Street, standing in front of an old-fashioned camera, giggling like a couple in the first blush of romance. 'You look good together.' The old photographer says.

A few flashes and laughs later and they are climbing back into the car. Suddenly a worried look appears on Ziad's face. 'Rima, I want to talk to you about something.'

'Now what?'

'It's not safe in Gaza anymore. I need to leave, Rima. And soon. I'm going to find a way for you to leave too.'

Rima doesn't even pause for breath. 'But I don't even have a passport, Ziad! How am I meant to get a permit or a coordination without a damn passport? You know I've been waiting for confirmation of my citizenship ever since we were 'returned' to Gaza.' Then she stops and realises what he means by 'not safe anymore'.

'Oh god, Ziad, what did you do?'

'I know you don't have travel papers but my friends will help you.'

'I don't want to, Ziad. We're not even married yet. My parents would never let us leave.'

'But we're engaged.'

'Are you new to this place or something?' Rima mocks him. 'Do you not know the scandal that would cause for my parents?'

A fresh silence fills the car.

'Rima, sing to me.'

'What?' He is still capable of surprising her, she thinks. 'But you don't like songs anymore!'

'I love everything you do, you're the only link to who I was.'

'Your father had a beautiful voice, Ziad!'

'Forget about him. He made his mistakes.'

'Don't say that. Your father was a great fighter.'

'But he didn't pray, and he smoked too much; drank alcohol. He believed in a freedom that wasn't his to believe in.'

'So? We all believe in our own salvation. We need to. All I know is that your father was honest, and patient, and he made sacrifices. He was a believer in the cause. Where do you get these distorted ideas from, Ziad? This isn't you speaking.'

'You've started to resemble Gaza,' he responded.

'Meaning?'

'It's like the sea washes everything away with you,' he bangs on the steering wheel. 'Why should you forgive what God doesn't?'

'Because I am not God. How should I know what God forgives and what God doesn't forgive? How do you know? All I have is the courage of my own convictions.'

Ziad's driving becomes erratic, cutting in and out of lanes, thoughtlessly. He floors the gas pedal and flexes his grip on the steering wheel. When he launches into his next rant, the wheel slips, and the car verges one way then the other, as he lets go to gesticulate every point.

'Tell me Rima: I believed in communism. I inherited Marx's doctrines from my father. I smoked cigars, wore a chain around my neck, let my shirt be unbuttoned down to the chest. I made a spectacle of my youth and masculinity. I even got myself arrested by the Israelis, and spent a few unforgettable months being tortured and freezing half to death in the prisons. I stood up for my principles and for my liberty. So tell me: where is the land my father promised would be mine again? It's getting further and further away. Peace has escaped. Hope has fled. All we can to do is return to God's teachings.'

Ziad pushes the car even faster.

'Stop,' Rima screams, 'please Ziad.'

At which point they do, crashing into a signpost indicating the direction to a nearby mosque.

Ziad sits in the drivers' seat crying into his beard. 'Rima, I feel totally alone. I've been so afraid since my father died. There is nothing left for me in this country.'

'What about me? I'm here.' He lets her embrace him, and they hold each other for a moment. Then he tries to start the car. As the car reverses off the pavement, the front bumper drops into the road. When Ziad returns from packing it into the boot, Rima has a twinkle in her eye.

'Ziad, let's go to Samarland Beach where we sat that night, all those years ago. Before your father died. I've missed the moonlight we sat under that night. We need that back in our lives.' Ziad smiles and takes her hand in his, steering the car back onto the road with the other one. Despite its new hissing, and the steam coming from the bonnet, the car feels normal again as they turn into a dark side street.

But then it is all over, and Ziad knows it. Above them is blinding light and the thunderous noise of an Apache. Before Rima can even process what's going on, Ziad has disengaged the engine, leapt out, and thrown himself under a pile of crates. The car carries on moving a few yards and she is still fiddling with her seatbelt when she hears his words, over the thunder of the blades.

'Rima get out!'

'I can't,' she cries, realising fear is what's making her so slow.

'They're going to fire!'

Somehow she manages to get far enough out of the car to be blown clear when it eventually explodes, scattering flames onto the tarmac on all sides.

For a moment they lie still in the street, on opposite sides of the car, gazing across at each other through its burning undercarriage. The helicopter's searchlight lights up Rima's face for what seems like an age, until she starts to move, at which point it crosses back to the car, still on fire, then back to Rima. Once it finally sets off, taking the blades' cacophony with it, Ziad slowly gets to his feet and staggers across to help Rima up. They steady themselves for a moment, and realise the streets are empty, just as that beach at the end of the road will be empty.

They reach Samarland Beach just as the sun is setting. They sit down on the sea wall, in their old spot, and draw each other closer, to contain their warmth. No gap can be seen between them this time as they watch the moon taking its cue from the sun, rising and trailing its glistening tails over the surface of a sea that won't sleep.

'You know, you're like the first day of spring,' he says.

'My face is all bloody and scratched.'

'You're beautiful,' he laughs, taking her into his own scratched and bloodstained arms.

'Ziad, my love. Let's not leave.'

About the Author

NAYROUZ QARMOUT is a Palestinian author and women's rights campaigner. Born in Damascus in 1984, she returned to the Gaza Strip as part of the 1994 Israeli-Palestinian Peace Agreement. Her short story 'The Sea Cloak' was first published in *The Book of Gaza* (2014), and she has written screenplays for several short films dealing with women's rights. Her political, social and literary articles have also appeared in numerous newspapers and magazines.

About the Translators

PERWEEN RICHARDS is a literary translator from the Arabic. She attended the Translate at City summer school in London in 2016, and was one of two winners of the school's annual translation competition, sponsored by Comma Press. Her translations have also appeared in *Banthology: Stories from Unwanted Nations* (Comma Press, 2018). *The Sea Cloak* is her first book-length translation.

CHARIS OLSZOK (née Bredin) is a Lecturer in Modern Arabic Literature and Culture, and a Bye-Fellow and Director of Studies for King's College, University of Cambridge. She has an MA in Arabic Literature and a PhD from SOAS, which looked at animals in modern Libyan fiction. She has translated a number of fiction excerpts for *Banipal Magazine* and several pieces for Darf Publishers.

ALSO AVAILABLE FROM COMMA PRESS...

Thirteen Months of Sunrise

Rania Mamoun

'A phenomenal, exacting collection'
– Preti Taneja

A young woman sits by her father's deathbed, lamenting her failure to keep a promise to him...

A struggling writer walks every inch of the city in search of inspiration, only to find it is much closer than she imagined...

A girl collapses from hunger at the side of the road and is rescued by the most unlikely of saviours...

In this powerful, debut collection of stories, Rania Mamoun expertly blends the real and imagined to create a rich, complex and moving portrait of contemporary Sudan. From painful encounters with loved ones to unexpected new friendships, Mamoun illuminates the breadth of human experience and explores, with humour and compassion, the alienation, isolation and estrangement that is urban life.

'A stunning collection, remarkable for its sweet clarity of voice and startling depictions of the marginalised and the destitute. With mastery, Rania Mamoun reaches straight into the heartbeat of her subject matter, laying bare humanity in all its tenderness and tenacity.' – Leila Aboulela, author of *Elsewhere Home*

Translated from the Arabic by Elisabeth Jaquette.

ISBN: 978-1-91097-439-1
£9.99

Palestine + 100

Edited by Basma Ghalayini

'Bold, brilliant and inspiring'
– *Bidisha*

Palestine + 100 poses a question to twelve Palestinian writers: what might your country look like in the year 2048 – a century after the tragedies and trauma of what has come to be called the Nakba? How might this event – which, in 1948, saw the expulsion of over 700,000 Palestinian Arabs from their homes – reach across a century of occupation, oppression, and political isolation, to shape the country and its people? Will a lasting peace finally have been reached, or will future technology only amplify the suffering and mistreatment of Palestinians?

Covering a range of approaches – from SF noir, to nightmarish dystopia, to high-tech farce – these stories use the blank canvas of the future to reimagine the Palestinian experience today. Along the way, we encounter drone swarms, digital uprisings, time-bending VR, peace treaties that span parallel universes, and even a Palestinian superhero, in probably the first anthology of science fiction from Palestine ever.

Featuring: Talal Abu Shawish, Tasnim Abutabikh, Selma Dabbagh, Emad El-Din Aysha, Samir El-Youssef, Saleem Haddad, Anwar Hamed, Majd Kayyal, Mazen Maarouf, Abdalmuti Maqboul, Ahmed Masoud & Rawan Yaghi

ISBN: 978-1-91097-444-5
£9.99